Things Liars Say

A #ThreeLittleLies novella

sara ney

THINGS LIARS SAY

Copyright © 2015 Sara Ney

All Rights Reserved

All rights reserved. No part of this publication may be reproduced, distributed, or transmitted in any form or by any means, including photocopying, recording, or other electronic or mechanical methods, without the prior written permission of the author, except in the case of brief quotations embodied in critical reviews and certain other noncommercial uses permitted by copyright law. For permission requests or comments, write to the author at:

Sara Ney, Author

saraneyauthor@yahoo.com

prologue

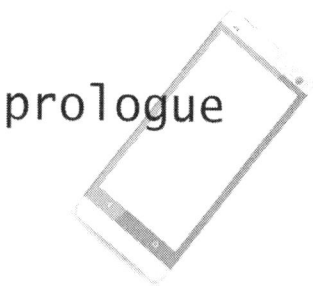

Greyson

The lie started off innocently enough, and obviously I never meant to get caught up in it—but then again, isn't that what *everyone* says when they lie?

Wait! No. Don't answer that.

Flipping my laptop open, I hit the power button and wait for it to boot, the soft familiar humming of the fan, CD drive, and modem stirring my computer to life, and shuffle the papers stacked in front of me.

I take a bite of the apple on my food tray, chewing slowly as I scan the meeting agenda on the table in front of me and my friends look on.

We're gathered in the university's dining hall for a quick lunch meeting on campus—the only time this week I could get my committee together in one spot at a time that worked for everyone.

"Rachel," I say across the cafeteria table. "Did you remember to call the catering company?"

My sorority sister gives me a victorious smile. "Yup. They have us booked for the third, and we have a tasting on the twenty-ninth at four thirty. It should have updated your calendar in Outlook."

I click open my Outlook and scroll through the calendar to the dates Rachel mentioned. "Excellent. There it is." I cross *catering* off my list and chew on the end of my BIC pen. "Jemma, are we all set with the silent auction donations?"

"Roger that, Greyson. I have ten alumnae lined up for baskets, and another thirteen parents who donated cash, totaling eight hundred dollars. We should be all set once we get everything purchased to put the baskets together."

"What other things do you have left for those?"

"You know, clear cello bags for the baskets, the wicker baskets themselves, labels… Those sorts of things."

"Who's going to be running the auction?" My pen hovers above the blank *auctioneer* spot on my agenda.

"You, Beth, and I can pull the silent-auction sheets at the end of the night."

I nod, crossing both *auction* and *donations* off my list.

"Ariel? Entertainment?"

Ariel, a tall brunette with a serious expression, pulls out an Excel spreadsheet and drums on it with her forefinger. "It looks like Cara put the deposit down for the DJ last week. He's scheduled to arrive a full hour before we start setting up the room so he can get all his equipment in the building without interruptions. I sent him a list of requested songs last night, so we should be good to go."

"As long as Vanessa doesn't request any of those group dances." Jemma snorts.

"Ugh. I hate 'The Electric Slide.'" Ariel laughs. "Should I add that to the do-not-play list?"

"Nah. Because you and I both know if the DJ plays it, you're going to run out onto the dance floor…"

Ariel sighs. "Probably."

I look down at my list and tap a pen to my chin. "So all we have to talk about yet is ticket sales. And getting everyone to sign the guest release waivers for liability."

I pull the form out of a file folder and slide it across the table to Catherine, one of three sisters in the sorority who are pre-law. She scans it with narrowed, articulate eyes and gives a curt nod when she reaches the last paragraph. "Looks great. Solid." Her lips curve into a smirk. "I like the addendum about recovering losses if property damage to the venue occurs by a guest. Good thinking."

Jemma snorts. "Remember what happened last year with Amanda Q's date? He ripped out an entire fern from the foyer of the hotel then threw up in the pot." We all laugh. "To add insult to injury, she snuck him out and then lied about it. Like there weren't security cameras everywhere."

Catherine gives a rueful shake of the head, disappointed we weren't able to charge anyone damages, and says, "Right. But since he hadn't signed a waiver, we couldn't charge him for the damage."

"Thank God it was just a few bags of potting soil…"

"But still. She shouldn't have left us hanging."

"Yeah, that was shitty."

Rachel turns to me with raised eyebrows. "Speaking of dates… Inquiring minds want to know: who is Greyson Keller bringing to the Philanthropy Gala this year?"

I shake my head. "I don't have time to worry about a date, you guys. I've been up to my eyeballs in Gala preparations."

"Don't you have to bring a date?" Jemma asks. "As the Philanthropy Chairwoman, you're the hostess this year."

I fiddle with my laptop's power cord and avoid her eyes. "What's your point?"

"Oh, come on, what's his name?" Rachel waves a limp french fry in my face from her lunch tray to get my attention. "Focus here; this stuff is important."

I finally look up, giving my blonde head a shake. "Who says there has to be a guy?"

"Please, there's *always* a guy…" Rachel's voice trails off.

"Just tell us who it is." Catherine prods quietly. Cajoling.

"Spit it out. We're going to find out eventually."

No, you're really not.

Jemma looks me dead in the eyes. "Yes. We are."

What the... Okay, that was freaky. And it occurs to me that they're acting like a gang of unruly hyenas and aren't going to let the subject die until I give them a reason to.

"I-I'd rather not say," I stutter. "We, uh, *just* started dating. It's only been one date. Besides, he's hardly Gala material."

"What the heck does that even mean?" Jemma scoffs. "Hardly Gala material? If he has a pulse, he's Gala material."

"One date?" Ariel drops her pen on the table. "Why did you feel that wasn't worth mentioning? Why haven't we at least heard about this guy before?"

"I don't want to jinx it?"

"Are you asking us or telling us?" Catherine's eagle eyes are unnerving, and I look away.

"Are you bringing him to the Gala?"

I take another bite of apple and respond with a mouthful. "I don't know yet. He might have... a... game?"

"Game?" Jemma's eyes get wide and excited. "Ooh, what is he, an athlete? Which sport?"

Great question, Jemma. I'll let you know when I figure it out myself. Everyone leans in closer for my answer, and I resist the urge to roll my eyes.

"He, uh… He's…" *Honestly, people. Why do you care so much?* Of course, I don't actually say this out loud.

"Oh, come on, Greyson. Don't get all secretive on us. It's not like we're going to stalk him on social media."

A few of them exchange telling, stealthy glances. What a bunch of freaking liars. The first thing they'll do when they leave this meeting is look for him on Facebook. Twitter. Bumble app… wherever—my point is, they would absolutely social media stalk him. I mean, if he existed.

I lie again.

"Fine. His name is…" I look around the room, my hazel eyes scanning the room, the food posters and the advertising signs adorning the walls. One for fresh, cold Farm Fresh California Milk jumps out at me. California. For some reason, it sticks out at me.

California. *Cal.*

"His name is uh, Cal, um… Cal."

"Cal?"

"That's right," I lie. "Yup. Cal."

"Cal? Cal what? What's his last name?"

Jesus, Rachel. Let it go!

I look at her dumbly. Crap. "His last name?"

"Grey, you're being *really* weird about this."

Again, my eyes scan the dining hall, landing on a girl who just happens to be in my economics class—and I just happened to have borrowed notes from her. Brianna Thompson.

Thompson it is.

"Sorry, I just zoned out for a second. His last name is, um, Thompson?"

"Asking or telling?"

"Telling." I give my head a firm nod. "Yup. Thompson. His last name is Thompson."

Cal Thompson. I roll the name around in my mind, deciding that I like it. Sounds believable.

Legit.

The lie works, because eventually they leave me alone and we go back to our meeting agenda, finish our committee work, and finish our lunch.

An apprehensive knot forms in the pit of my stomach as I swallow the last bite of my spinach chicken wrap.

Little do I know, the lies that so easily rolled off my tongue today will soon become entirely too real.

chapter one

Calvin

"Cal. You there, man? You've gotta come check this out," my roommate Mason calls from his bedroom, the music blaring from his Bose sound system. Combined with the background noise of the television in the living room, the noise pollution almost drowns out his request.

Unfortunately for me, I'm not that lucky, and he calls for me again. "Come here, man. Seriously."

Christ, he's a pain in the ass. "Hold your fucking horses; I'm in the middle of something," I call back.

Yeah. I'm in the middle of something: stuffing my face with a sub sandwich and washing it down with a cold beer. I swipe the other half of my sub off the counter and wrap it in a napkin before sauntering, unhurriedly, to Mason's end of the apartment. I lean nonchalantly against his doorjamb, taking another huge bite of sandwich and chewing slowly.

"What."

He cranes his beefy neck towards me in the doorway, irritated. "I said come check this out. Jeez. Why are you standing there? Where's your sense of urgency?"

Rolling my eyes, I venture in a few feet. "If this is more porn, I'm going to be fucking pissed."

"Whatever. Trust me, this is worth our time."

"Our? No. Don't say our." Skeptically, I sidle up next to his desk chair, and he turns his computer monitor on its base to face me. He has his Twitter feed pulled up, and his beefy forefinger pokes the screen, pointing to a particular Tweet.

It's too damn bad I can't focus on anything with his loud, crap R&B music blasting out of his speakers.

"Would you turn that shit down a notch?"

Mason sighs but clicks a few buttons with his mouse, shutting the radio off. "Okay. So, check it. I follow my cousin Jemma, who goes to State, on Instagram and Reddit and shit."

I roll my eyes. "Okay." *Get to the point.*

"Anyway, Jemma is in this sorority, right? Hottest chicks on campus. I went once to visit when they had family weekend—don't ask me why." My roommate pauses, and for a second I'm hopeful he won't continue talking.

But guess what? He tells me why.

"My Aunt Cindy—Jemma's mom—had her panties in a twist about everyone going. Come to think of it, she probably wanted me there to hook me up with a nice girl and—"

I emit a very irritated and exasperated sigh. "Jesus Christ, Mase, where are you going with all this? Make your fucking point."

"Sorry. My point is, I follow Jemma on Twitter, right?" *Oh my effing God.* "Her sorority has this big fancy dance thing coming up. They do it every year. Anyway, some *dude* named Grey must be helping them plan this event, right? Cause it's a big deal. And see here?" Mason stabs his index finger on the computer monitor again, pointing to another Tweet.

"I swear to all that is holy, if you don't make your point I'm going to lose my shit."

"Some Grey guy tweeted *your* name as his *date*. Check it."

I lean in to scan the screen closely, my brows furrowing into an angry line when I read the tweet in front of me.

Holy shit, the bastard is right.

@JemmaGemini Tweeted: Theta Gala season is here! Host with the most @grey_vkeller and date @calthompson3192 are now selling tickets! Get yours here (click on link) #state #sorority #philanthropy #ThetaGala15

My fists clench at my side. "What. The. Actual. *Fuck*."

"Wait, hold on—there's more. That was just yesterday." Mason moves his mouse around, clicking until the screen scrolls down. Up pop's Grey Keller's profile and history. "Check this one out." He points to the monitor.

"I'd be able to if you'd get your fucking finger out of the way," I snap, leaning in closer until my face is inches from the screen. "I can't see."

"You can ask nicely, you know…"

My jaw clenches shut tightly, and Mason moves his finger.

We peer at the Tweets, heads bent together.

@Grey_VKeller Tweeted: missed you @calthompson3192 at #StateTailgate knock them dead at your game, honey buns! #thompsonforthewin

@Grey_VKeller Tweeted: nothing beats @starbucks and @calthompson3192 on these cold rainy days #blahs #raingoaway #soylatte #boyfriend #boyfriendsweater #hugs

@Grey_VKeller Tweeted: What @calthompson3192 needs is a #queereyeforthestraightguy as he tries on suits for #ThetaGala15

There are more, but Mason is reading them out loud over my shoulder, and his commentary is starting to get on my last nerve.

"Did that hashtag say Queer Eye for the Straight Guy?" he asks the silence. "Hey. What's worse than having a stalker?" Mason asks with a smirk, answering his own question when I give him a dark scowl. "Being stalked by a *guy*. Hey. Do you think he's come to any of our matches and we just didn't know it?"

"How did you find these?"

"I told you, my cousin Jemma. She retweeted these, and even though it's a bogus Twitter account—I checked—your name still stuck out at me."

"That is so messed up."

"Sucks to be you, man."

"Shut the fuck up, Mason."

"I'm just saying. He's out there watching you, and you didn't even know it. That's gross, dude."

That's the very last thing I want to hear, so I prod my roommate sharply in the shoulder with my elbow, narrowly missing his head.

"Shut the fuck up already!" I repeat irritably. "I can't hear myself think."

"But I turned the radio off."

"I meant *shut your yap*."

"Sorry. Just thinking out loud." Then he mumbles, "You're being a real bitch about this."

"Not. Helping."

"Noted." But then he adds, "But you admit he could be watching you at our games."

I narrow a steely gaze at him. "How do we even know it's a guy?" Great. Now I'm using the royal *we*.

He shoots me an impatient look. "What are you, a moron? Grey is a guy's name, bruh. That's how we know it's a guy."

@Grey_VKeller Tweeted:

@calthompson3192 counting down the days until #ThetaGala15 and I see your handsome face

@Grey_VKeller Tweeted:

@calthompson3192 last night was wonderful. Wish you lived closer so I could see you more often #sexy #stud

"This Grey dude must be blind," Mason says beside me, and I give him another nudge—this time in the back of the head. "Ow, what the hell, man?"

I grunt unhappily.

"You could break a mirror is all I'm saying." Mason mumbles, rubbing his neck.

"Fuck you."

###

My fist comes down like a hammer on the flimsy wooden door that at one time might have been painted blue but currently looks like shit. In fact, with one swift pull I could probably yank the whole thing off its rusty hinges.

Hovering behind like a couple of chicken shits are my roommates, Aaron Buchanan and Mason, standing down on the loose concrete slab next to the porch. They accompanied me for one reason and one reason only: a good laugh.

Let's not forget to trail along out of perverse curiosity, and if necessary, to pull me off the useless bastard I just drove forty-five minutes to confront.

And beat the piss out of.

"Thompson, you've knocked four times. Maybe there's no one home," Mason rationalizes, checking his phone for messages. His thumb glides over his smartphone, his mouth widening into smirk. He begins tapping away furiously even as he adds, "Time to give it a rest."

I narrow my predatory gaze at the blue door. "Oh, there's definitely someone home. I hear music."

Aaron crosses his bulky arms and frowns. "Well, don't beat the fucking door down. Take it easy."

I shoot him a glare over my shoulder and crack my knuckles. "That's easy for you to say. Some guy isn't impersonating your boyfriend on every social media site known to man."

The thought riles me up, and I curl my hand into a fist, giving the plywood door another hollow rap with my knuckles. "*Come out, come out, wherever you are.* Open the damn door, you little pissant," I chant to myself. "I don't have all fucking day."

"Dude, you sound like a psychopath." Mason laughs without lifting his head from his phone. He nudges Aaron. "Check it out. Sasha Baldwin just sent me a picture of her ass."

My last blasted knock does the trick, because suddenly the music cuts out inside the house, I hear some rustling, and a feminine voice shouts, "Coming!" This is followed by the low sound of hastening footpads advancing towards the entrance, the deadbolt turning, and the door flying open.

"Sorry 'bout that. We didn't hear the door. Obviously." A tall brunette stares curiously through the storm door, a bright smile pasted on her pretty face, hand propped on her slim waist.

She looks at me, eyes darting from me to Aaron and Mason, who are suddenly standing at attention. If possible, the brunette's mega-watt smile widens. "Well, *hello* there. Can I help you?"

Head tipped to the side, I regard her critically as she studies the three of us back with open interest, and I can see her trying to place us in her mind. Trying to figure out if she's seen us before or met us around campus. Or at a party.

No such luck, sweetheart. Today is not your lucky day.

In black yoga pants and a large, baby-blue State sweatshirt, her dark brown hair is pulled back into a loose ponytail. Basically, she looks like the girl next door: fresh faced, normal, and nice.

And did I mention normal? As in *not harboring a known stalker*.

But as we all know, looks can be deceiving, and those keen brown eyes glowing towards my idiot roommates are no exception. Peeved, I want to shake the shit out of them both for being captivated by this pretty, attractive girl. Captivated by her deceptively innocent face—as if she couldn't possibly be a mental person. As if there were a scarcity of pretty girls on our own college campus for them to ogle. There is not.

I angrily snap my fingers in their direction. "Guys, focus. You don't get to drool over this one."

They both have the decency to look embarrassed, and when I catch Mason ascending the stoop, I shove him back down onto the sidewalk. I roll my eyes, turning towards the door.

"Is your boyfriend home?" I cut to the chase.

"My *what*?" Her nose curls up. "I don't have a boyfriend." She presses forward, closer to the screen, and looks out into the yard—at freaking Mason, who's blushing.

Jesus. What a clusterfuck.

"I'm looking for a guy that lives here."

She tips her head at me, confused. "Erm, maybe you have the wrong house?"

I look down at the address on the screen of my smartphone. "No. This is the address I was given."

"Given by… whom?"

I thumb my hand in Mason's direction. "His cousin Jemma."

The brunette's eyes narrow. "Jemma? Oh *really*."

At that moment, I know exactly what she's thinking: the moment this blue door closes, this Jemma chick is going to get her ass chewed. I have a sister, and I've seen this look a million times.

The brunette looks me over from head to toe, then top to bottom, memorizing the color of my eyes, measuring my height, the color of my hair, and any distinguishing scars or birthmarks. Probably so she can profile me to the police.

Great.

CSI Barbie crosses her arms. "Who was it you said you were looking for?"

"I didn't."

"Are you serious?" The brunette snorts sarcastically, going from pleasant to defensive. "Look, I don't know who you think you are or who it is you're looking for, but there are no guys living here—"

"—I'm looking for Greyson Keller. Is he here?"

Her expression is priceless: eyes wide as saucers, eyebrows shot up into her dark hairline, and mouth agape. A dimple threatens to press into her right cheek.

Busted. I've found my guy.

"Greyson *Keller*?" The girl laughs, tipping her head back. "Oh, this is gonna be good." She looks me up and down, a weird expression on her face that I can't quite put my finger on: amusement. Curiosity. Glee?

Self-consciously, I fold my arms across my broad chest. "Oh, *Greyson* is here all right. Let me go get, uh… *him*. Give me one minute?"

She starts to close the door behind her but peeks her head around it, adding, "Stay there; do *not* go anywhere."

I roll my eyes. "Whatever, make it quick." My fists clench and unclench at my sides, warming up and impatient to get the show on the road.

The door slams shut, but I clearly hear a muted, "Grey! Someone's at the door for you!" This announcement is followed by, "You're what? Oh, okay." Then a muffled, "Make it snappy, chica. You are *so* not going to want to miss this."

Chica?

Then I hear, "Grey, hurry up. Huh? Well, hurry. Yeah, yeah, you already said that."

Soon, from somewhere inside the house, one feminine voice is joined by another—this one pleasant and sweet—responding with a sing-songy, "Give me a second! Be right there!"

Mason appears beside me. "Do my ears deceive me, or was that another chick's voice?" He slips his cell into the pocket of his low-rise jeans.

"That was *definitely* another chick's voice," Aaron agrees, stepping closer to the house.

The door unlatches from within, the knob turns, and the blue front door is pulled open once again on its rusty hinges. Natural sunlight hits the girl who appears in the doorway like a spotlight, her long blonde hair shining around her head like a halo.

Momentarily shocked, I take a step back, and she steps closer. Like an idiot, I stare. "I'm looking for Greyson Keller."

"Yes?"

I roll my eyes. "Not *you*, sweetie, your boyfriend. Go grab him for me so I can bash his face in."

The blonde bites her lower lip and laughs. "I'm Greyson. As much as I hate asking, can I… help you?"

"No you're not." Confused, my brows drop into a deep V, and I turn back towards my roommates. They shrug uselessly. "Uh, I'm here for Greyson. Greyson *Keller*?"

"Found her. That's me." Her pouty pink mouth gives me a lopsided grin, full of straight white teeth.

"You can keep saying my name as long as you want, but no one else is walking out that front door."

"You're a girl," Aaron blurts out.

"Aren't you observant?" The blonde's expressive hazel eyes shine with amusement as she spreads her hands wide at her waist with a light laugh. "Mmmhmm. Last time I checked, I still had all my girly parts."

And what girly parts they were: hands sweeping airily around the flouncy skirt of a tight, feminine sundress, long tan legs accentuated by the short hemline flaring out around her hips.

Around her tan legs. Shit, did I already say that?

"Tighthead, if *that's* Greyson Keller, you are so screwed," Mason mutters into my ear from behind, poking me in the back with his bony elbow. "Walk away, man, before you look like an even bigger douche."

I scowl and elbow him in the gut and am satisfied when he grunts. "Shut the fuck up, Mase. You're not helping."

Not to mention, this is all his goddamn fault. He couldn't have done a little more thorough recon work before raising a red flag?

Fuck.

Running a hand through my hair, I give Greyson a once-over from under hooded eyes.

Long, light blond hair falls over her bare shoulders in one of those sexy, messy French braid things, and freckles lightly dance across the bridge of her straight, pert nose. Her chest rises up and down breathlessly, her cheeks taking on a rosy hue as she lets me study her.

God, she's... she's gorgeous. Not the ordinary, pretty kind of gorgeous. No. She's *make you want to weep into your beer* breathtakingly beautiful.

Or, at least, she is to me.

Fuckity fuck fuck.

"Is... there something I can help you with?" She's biting down on a pink, pouty lower lip. "Are you fraternity pledges?"

I glance at her friend hovering from behind in the living room, hanging on our every word. She looks amused, entertained, and entirely too pleased with herself. Like a gleeful toddler who didn't get caught stealing a piece of candy.

Bitch.

CSI Barbie's laughing gaze shifts to the nitwits standing behind me with unconcealed interest, and I groan. Suddenly, I'm not too thrilled with the idea of confronting *this* version of Greyson Keller in public. In front of our friends.

I clear my throat. "Is there somewhere we can talk? Privately?"

Greyson nods slowly as her roommate shrugs in acquiescence. The brunette stares me down. "I'm blowing my rape whistle if you're not back on this porch in ten minutes, asshole."

She shoots me a cheeky grin.

"Maybe we'll take a quick walk?" Beautiful, blonde, and *female* Greyson Keller puts her arm around her friend's waist. "I'll stay within shooting distance," she teases with a glance at me. "Okay?"

I give a jerky nod. "Yeah. Okay."

"Let me grab my shoes."

She releases her friend's waist and disappears, returning several moments later and a few inches taller, pushing through the screen door and stepping out onto the porch.

Her hot-pink painted toes peek out from a pair of cork wedge sandals, legs going on for miles. Her sundress is everything it should be: tight bodice dipping into a V, giving me the perfect view of her respectable cleavage. The dress is tied in the back with a bow around her small waist, and as she smiles up at me, I swallow back a groan.

Why is she wearing a dress cut like that? Why does she look so goddamn cute? Was she about to go somewhere? Shit, why does she have to look so damn good? Why couldn't she have been fugly? *Why couldn't she have been a guy?*

Why the fuck, why?

Then at least I wouldn't feel so guilty for wanting to pummel her ass.

I am hating myself right now.

Greyson leads me to the sidewalk and takes a right once we hit the pavement. "Let's head this way. It leads to a dead end."

I cram my large hands deep into the pocket of my jeans.

"So…" Her voice hitches in a silent question.

We walk for a few yards before I grow a pair of balls big enough to speak. "Here's the deal. I came here to beat the shit out of you," I blurt out. "I thought you were some dude stalking me on Twitter and Facebook. A guy."

Gasping, she stops in her tracks, shocked. "Why? What! *Why?*" she sputters. "I don't understand. Help me understand."

"On Twitter, are you Grey underscore Keller, Theta Rho?"

She hesitates, turning to face me, biting down on her lower lip. "Yes."

God, I wish she hadn't just given me that look.

"I'm Cal Thompson."

"*What?*" she shouts. Understanding shines in her eyes, and she takes a stumbling step back onto the grassy curbside. "You can't be!"

"Oh, I assure you, sweetheart—I am."

"B-but," she sputters, a blush making her chest, neck, and face red. "I made you up!" A hand clamps over her mouth as she moans. "Oh my God, this cannot be happening to me right now."

"Yet here I am."

I pull out my wallet and produce both my driver's license and student ID, tossing them at her. Because she wasn't expecting the onslaught, she misses, and the identification cards flutter to the concrete sidewalk. "There. Take a gander."

I know it's rude, but frankly, I don't give a shit.

With trembling hands, she bends at the knee demurely, sliding a hand along the folds of her skirt to preserve her modesty, and reaching for the ID's, her long fingers plucking them off the ground.

She studies them both as she stands, her expression crestfallen.

"How? Oh my god, C-Cal. I'm so, *so* sorry. And embarrassed." Her hand flies to her mouth. "So embarrassed," she repeats with a whisper. Grey's full bottom lip quivers, and she glances back towards her house nervously. "My friends don't know I made you up. My friends are the *reason* I made you up."

Aaron, Mason, and her roommate—all within *shooting* distance— watch us from the porch fifty yards away, not even bothering to hide their interest.

Shit. I don't want her to cry—even if what she did was fifty shades of fucked up.

"Explain it to me, then."

She nods slowly.

Greyson

I cannot believe this is happening.

The guy standing in front of me is so freaking angry, a shocking myriad of expressions dancing across his face: Perturbed. Confused. Stunned. Pissed off.

He looks like he came to beat the *crap* out of someone and is disappointed he isn't going to have the opportunity.

I study the planes of his hard face as he walks beside me, a fresh bruise discoloring the rise of his high cheekbone just beneath his left eye, but oddly made less severe by his deep tan. I conclude that he must spend an excessive amount of time outdoors if the sun-kissed tips of the sandy blonde hair curling up from under the lid of his ball cap are any indication.

I take in his eyes: dark pools of cobalt blue made harsh and unforgiving by the severe slashes of dense eyebrows above them. Square jaw with a day's growth of beard surrounding a full, downturned mouth.

Black stitches mend the gash marring his busted-up lower lip.

Tall—maybe six foot one—with lean hips, I can't resist letting my eyes wander down the length of him. They take in the broad, sculpted chest, straining against a tight gray Ivy League t-shirt—a shirt that leaves nothing to the imagination, as evidenced by the defined pec muscles outlined by the sheer threadbare fabric.

If Cal's shoulders are a thing of beauty, then his arms are a thing of *art*, dense and firm and ripped. A large, intricate tattoo snakes up the tendons of his tricep, twisting up his bicep and disappearing under the sleeve of his shirt. Tan, powerful biceps any girl would want to curl her fingers around with a contented, dreamy sigh.

They're arms a girl would blissfully want wrapped around her in a crowded bar. Out in public. Or, let's be honest, a tangle of sheets.

I can't decide if he's handsome or good-looking or not—not by today's definition of classically handsome, anyway. He's too severe. His nose has been broken too many times, his skin has too many scars, but there *is* something about him that I find ruggedly appealing. I just can't put my finger on what that something could be.

However, decision made: I like what I see.

A lot.

"Hmmm." I must have muttered this out loud, because he looks over at me and catches me horn dogging him. I open my mouth to say something then clamp it shut. *Take a deep breath, Greyson. Just take a deep breath and spit it out.*

He deserves an explanation.

"Alright. When I tell you how I ended up faking a boyfriend, I hope you don't..." I wave a hand through the air, listlessly. Nervously. "Judge me too harshly. Please."

We continue walking, reaching the dead end. Cal nods towards the opposite side of the deserted road, and together, we step off the curb and cross to the other side, continuing our meander back in the direction from which we came.

I take a deep breath and exhale.

"To start with, I'm the philanthropy chair of my sorority." He snorts, and I roll my eyes, quite used to non-Greek students mocking my sorority membership. "A philanthropy is a charitable organization we support through fundraising and donations."

I take another deep, shallow breath. "Anyway, this year we're throwing a big gala. The largest one we've put on, with the most number of attendees. It's been... really stressful. I have a committee, but you know how it is. Not everyone is committed. Not everyone pulls their weight. And with everything *else* we have to juggle..."

Cal listens silently as I continue, my explanation rapidly becoming a vent session.

"...school, grades, jobs, athletics. I don't expect you to care, but... you get the picture. Anyway, with all that being said, a few of them are, for lack of better words, boy crazy." I give him a sidelong glance, but he stoically faces forward. "All they want to talk about during the meetings are their dates for the gala, and they won't stop hounding *me* about who *I'm* bringing. So, yada, yada, yada, Cal Thompson."

As if that explained everything.

"Wait. Did you just use yada, yada, yada as your justification? Who *does* that?" Cal sputters a little, and stops short on the sidewalk, trying not to laugh but failing, emitting a short, deep bark.

"You don't like yada, yada, yada?" I shoot him a coy smile. "What's wrong with it?"

"You sound kind of crazy," he teases, his eyes crinkling at the corners with amusement. "I guess the bigger picture is, how the hell did you end up using *my* name? How did you hear about me? We're not even in the same stratosphere."

"Whoa, buddy, it's not like you're famous. Let's not get *too* full of ourselves." I hand him back the driver's license and student ID I've been holding and give a little shiver when our fingers touch.

"Trust me, I had no idea who you were. I pulled your name out of thin air. In fact, you could say I was inspired. There's a sign hanging in the dining hall for Farm Fresh California milk. *Cal*ifornia—Cal. See? So then my friends want a last name, and I'm scouring the room, I see this girl from my econ class, Brianna—"

"Thompson," we both say at the same time.

"Yes. Brianna Thompson." I laugh. "So, there you have it, the day Cal Thompson was born. Or in this case, invented."

"What about the tweets?"

"Well, my friend Jemma is a public relations major and is *all* about social media. She's Theta's PR and Marketing Chairwoman and the one who insisted on the live tweeting. Thinks it's more 'relevant.'" Yes, I use air quotes. "Jemma literally makes us Tweet during our meeting to get people excited, which is great! Good for her. I mean, I love her to death, but now it's getting obnoxious."

"Jemma is my roommate Mason's cousin—he follows her on Twitter."

"Ah. All the puzzle pieces come together." I keep walking and notice Cal checking out my legs. I pretend not to notice; my steps become jaunty. "What does Mason think of all this?"

He peels his eyes away and looks up, down the street towards my yard. "Mason and Aaron are dipshits and get a rise out of seeing me pissed off. They came today expecting a fight."

I ball my fists up and put up my dukes, bouncing on the heels of my four-inch wedges. "It's not too late!"

His dark blue eyes rake me up and down again appraisingly, but not in a creepy, pervy way. "Okay, Mayweather, cool it with your bad self." Cal considers me then, scratching his five o'clock shadow. "You know, I never thought I'd have my own personal stalker."

I laugh, relieved that he's making light of the situation. "Oh, please. If I were stalking you, you would know it. I'd have done a much better job creeping you out than a few measly tweets." I nudge him with my elbow conspiratorially, startled to realize I'm enjoying our banter and warming to the topic. "Maybe driven past your house… found a few of your classes… crafted myself a tiny Cal doll to cuddle at night…" I cross my arms and hug myself, pretending to squeeze a stuffed animal. "Um, yeah. *That* part might have sounded crazy."

"That. Sounded. Terrifying." He shivers. "Well, the weird thing is— it was actually a total fluke that anyone saw my name in your Tweets because Cal Thompson isn't even the name I use on any social media online. I haven't used that since high school."

"It isn't? Don't leave me in suspense. What's your real tag?"

He laughs. "Tighthead Thompson. Tighthead is a rugby thing."

That explains the gashes, scratches, and bruises.

"Ah. Rugby, huh? We don't have that on our campus."

"I'm sure there's an intramural league here somewhere. Most schools offer at least that. It's typically only played competitively at smaller schools, and some Ivy League schools."

"How long have you been playing?" I ask, feeling at ease with him and sincerely wanting to know more.

"Three years by accident." Cal stops on the sidewalk when we're standing across the street from my rental but makes no move to cross the street. "I played football for years and just got sick of it. I had a scholarship to a D1 school, but…" His sentence trails off with a shrug. "I just didn't want that kind of pressure."

I raise my eyebrows. "What did your parents say about you giving up a scholarship?"

"They're supportive; they want me to be happy."

"Wow, they sound great."

"The best," he agrees with a small grin, nodding towards my shoddy little house. "Okay, so… I guess this is you, then." He shoves his hands in his pockets, and we step down into the street to cross.

"I guess. And again, I'm so sorry. It was such a stupid, careless thing to do."

"Yes, but…" he concedes. "No harm done."

"Except the part where you came all this way to kick my ass," I point out gamely.

"Yeah," he agrees. "Except the part where I drove all this way to kick your ass." He gives me an expression full of longing, clearing his throat once his gaze hits my breasts and lingers there. He blushes and looks away. "I'm actually really disappointed I didn't get the chance."

"Well, thank you, then—for *not* whooping my butt. I'm sure I deserved it." I run a hand over my long blonde braid, and Cal's bright, fascinated eyes follow the motion, sending tingles up my spine. I want to do it again just to see his reaction. "And thank you for not being a total jerk."

"Don't get me wrong. I was really pissed."

"I'll bet…" I tap my chin, and his gaze hits my mouth. "But on the bright side, it was only an hour drive, and you gave your friends something to talk about, probably for *years*. Ugh. Years."

"A few years at *least*. But just look at how happy they are." Our friends are still gathered on the porch, watching us walk back into the yard, chatting happily yet eyeing Cal and me with avid curiosity.

"They're like little puppy dogs."

I giggle. "I can't even begin to imagine what they're going to say when they finally get you alone."

Cal laughs. "Your ears will be ringing, that's for sure."

"For years," I remind him.

"Okay, you little sneak. Who. Was. *That?*" My roommate Melody ambushes me as soon as the screen door closes and the guys pull away in Cal's big red pickup truck. I give him a jaunty little wave from behind the screen before stepping into Melody's eager web of inquisition.

"That was... Well, Mel. *That* was Cal Thompson."

"That was Cal Thompson? Seriously! Where the hell have you been hiding him?" She pauses, the truth setting in. "Wait. I'm confused. If that was your boyfriend, why was he acting like he didn't know who you were?"

"Because... he... Ugh. God, Mel, I'm an *idiot*. That's why." How do I explain this without sounding like a mental person?

"Grey. Just tell me the truth." Melody puts her hand on my shoulder. "I won't judge you, promise."

So I do.

I tell her everything.

chapter two

Calvin

As soon as the truck door slams shut, Aaron is half out of his seat, punching me in the arm. "Holy shit, Thompson, your stalker is fucking hot. Did you get her number?"

My hands white knuckle the steering wheel. "No." But I wanted to. God, how I wanted to.

Aaron looks at me like I've lost my goddamn mind. "Why the hell not?"

"Uh, because she's a fucking *stalker*," Mason responds.

"So?"

They're still bickering when I enter the off-ramp for the highway, and they're bickering forty minutes later when we pull up to our off-campus housing.

"Her roommate was smokin' hot too, and funny as shit. They're in a sorority, man. Sexy as hell."

Yeah, it is.

Aaron considers this information. "Way out of your league, bro."

"Don't kick a man when he's down," Mason chastises as we climb out of my truck.

Greyson

@Grey_VKeller @tightheadthompson *remember what I said about live tweeting during our meetings? It's happening. Right. Now.*

@tightheadthompson @grey_vkeller *So is this a pity tweet for the sake of your charade?* #ouch #feelings

@Grey_VKeller @tightheadthompson *Shhhhhh. No talking about the charade in public!* #partnersincrime

@tightheadthompson @grey_vkeller *people can read, you know* #notsubtle #publicforum

@Grey_VKeller @tightheadthompson *valid point*

@tightheadthompson @grey_vkeller *I'm usually always right, but I'll let this one slide because you're* #cute

@Grey_VKeller @tightheadthompson *are you flirting with me, Cal Thompson?* #causethatwouldbeawesome

@JemmaGemini @tightheadthompson *whoever you are, could you STOP Tweeting @grey_vkeller? We're trying to be PRODUCTIVE* #distraction #meeting #focus

@Grey_VKeller @tightheadthompson *I'm getting scolded* #momsaysicantplay

@tightheadthompson @grey_vkeller *speaking of charades, maybe I should just get your personal info—just to spare you from further public embarrassment* #gentleman

@Grey_VKeller @tightheadthompson *have your people contact my people* @JemmaGemini #giveMasonmyinfo

###

To: grevkeller0143@state.edu
From: cal.thompson04@smu.il.edu
Subject: Circling back

Greyson. Hey. Just wanted to make sure you're not beating yourself up over the whole lying, stalking thing. Because I'm over it and feel much safer knowing I could definitely take you out in a fight. I don't know why your friend would only give Mason your email address and not your cell phone number. – Cal

To: cal.thompson04@smu.il.edu
From: grevkeller0143@state.edu
Subject: Can't even say how sorry I am…

Calvin,

Your concern fills me with warm fuzzies. I'm taking it day-by-day, each day getting easier and easier to look myself in the mirror. That was sarcasm, by the way. I'm guessing the reason Jemma wouldn't give your roommate my cell is because you look ten kinds of crazy. You're big and scary, black eye and tattoos. Thank you for the email, though, and for not holding a grudge against my stupidity. I guess this means I owe you a favor. Grey

To: grevkeller0143@state.edu
From: cal.thompson04@smu.il.edu
Subject: Don't worry about it.

Greyson, no one has ever called me big and scary. Or ten kinds of crazy—at least not to my face. What does that even mean? And yeah, you owe me. Hell yeah you do. And don't call me Calvin. – Cal

To: cal.thompson04@smu.il.edu
From: grevkeller0143@state.edu
Subject: I'm stressed out and not thinking clearly?

Calvin,

Sorry for the delay. Speaking of ten kinds of crazy, things are REALLY crazy here. Only a few more weeks until our Gala, and I'm really trying to hold it together. We have one hundred and five tickets sold! I can hardly believe it. Confession: although it's a fundraiser, I kind of hope we don't sell any more! That's a ton of people! I want to go to the event and have SOME fun. Anyway, don't let me get started on all that... Tell me, what does a guy like you do in his free time? Grey

To: grevkeller0143@state.edu
From: cal.thompson04@smu.il.edu
Subject: What is this free time you speak of?

Grey, a guy like me? First of all, every time I see your name in this email, I *still* cannot believe you're a girl. LOL. My roommates haven't shut up about it, and I think Mason has a crush on your roomie. He can't stop talking about how smart and funny she is.

What do I do in my "free time"? My free time is probably spent a lot like yours: homework, studying, hanging with the guys. We like parties. And, as you know, we play Rugby. I've been Captain since last year, as a sophomore. What about you? What does Greyson "not a guy" Keller do in her free time? – Cal

To: cal.thompson04@smu.il.edu
From: grevkeller0143@state.edu
Subject: LAE (long-ass email)

Calvin (sorry, I can't seem to help myself),

Wow, Captain?! Impressive. I don't know much about Rugby except that the players are big, and they get black eyes and banged up a lot. And they drive big trucks. Other than that, I'm pretty clueless. In my "free time"—if you can call it that—I spend a lot of time with my sorority sisters. Home is a 5-hour drive away, so I stay on campus most of the time and don't go home often. My sorority sisters are my family. I like to read and dabble in writing (tweets ☺ haha). I don't mind hitting the bar scene every once in a while, but... guys are pretty *grabby*, and I can't stand that. Grey

PS: I also want to add that other than inventing the occasional fake boyfriend, I'm usually always very honest.

To: grevkeller0143@state.edu
From: cal.thompson04@smu.il.edu
Subject: Fake boyfriends are underrated

Grey, speaking of being very honest, I can *honestly* say I'm never intentionally been grabby with a woman. Although I don't mind a consensual handful of ass cheek. Was that TOO honest for you? Just testing the waters. – Cal

To: cal.thompson04@smu.il.edu
From: grevkeller0143@state.edu
Subject: No date is better than a blind date

Cal,

Is there such a thing as too honest? I'll ponder that... As far as ass grabbing goes, I guess I wouldn't mind it if the grabber was my date. Or my fake date. And since we're being honest, the only person who knows you don't exist—I mean, who knows you aren't really my boyfriend—is my roommate Melody. I do feel terrible lying, but we can't sit and talk about guys during our committee meetings. We get nothing done when we do. It drives my friends nuts that I'm single, and I do *not* want to be set up. Blind dates are the worst. Wouldn't you agree? Grey

To: grevkeller0143@state.edu
From: cal.thompson04@smu.il.edu
Subject: Use me up then spit me out.

So, what you're saying is, you still plan on using me so your friends don't try and set you up on a blind date? And yeah, I agree that those are the worst, although I've never been on one. Speaking of dating: I think it's rude you haven't asked my permission to use me. – Cal

To: cal.thompson04@smu.il.edu
From: grevkeller0143@state.edu
Subject: Request document submitted

Calvin, do I have your permission to use you as my fake boyfriend? Grey

To: grevkeller0143@state.edu
From: cal.thompson04@smu.il.edu
Subject: Request document received

Greyson, to answer that, I should probably have your cell phone number. – Cal

###

697-555-5155: *Grey, this is Cal. Thought it would be easier to text rather than email. What was your question again?*

Grey: *Calvin, took you long enough to ask for my phone number.*

Cal: *For the sake of convenience, it had to be done.*

Grey: *That's the story you're sticking with?*

Cal: *Yup, pretty much.*

Grey: *I guess I'll jump right to the negotiations then. Calvin, do I have your permission to use you as my fake boyfriend?*

Cal: *Let me think about it. This all seems so sudden... are you sure we're not rushing into things?*

Grey: *You're wittier than you look, Cal Thompson*

Cal: *THANKS! Shit. That felt like an insult. Or was it a compliment? Dammit.*

Grey: *LOL*

Cal: *LOL? Fucking rude is what you are. You're lucky you're an hour away.*

Grey: *Or you'd WHAT? Come kick my ass or something?*

Cal: *Or something.*

Grey: *So, do I have your permission?*

Cal: *Yes. But when I start feeling dirty and violated, I'm breaking up with you. Also, please don't tell anyone I "put out" on the first date.*

Grey: *I never kiss and tell...*

chapter three

To: grevkeller0143@state.edu
From: cal.thompson04@smu.il.edu
Subject: Gray skies and stormy weather.

Grey. This shitty, gray overcast day reminded me of you—but not in a bad way. How's it going over there at State? Had a rugby match this weekend, and I've been icing some seriously sore muscles for the past few days. It sucks. Can hardly move. I also have a cracked lip and another black eye—one that matches the shiner you saw last week. But it looks badass, so who am I to complain? I never did ask what your major is. Mine is business. Yawn. Boring, right? My dad owns a commercial construction company, and after working in the field a few years, I plan to take over when he retires. – Cal

To: cal.thompson04@smu.il.edu
From: grevkeller0143@state.edu
Subject: Grey the Procrastinator

Calvin,

Yes, I'm sticking with that moniker. For some reason, it pleases me knowing that you don't like it... Business is also my major, except I'm not sure which direction I want to take it. Unlike most of my friends, I don't really know what to do with a business degree. Choosing a major was one of the toughest decisions I've ever had to make. I actually waited to declare until I absolutely had to. I have passion for a lot of things. Like event planning and team building. Is that weird? Grey

To: grevkeller0143@state.edu
From: cal.thompson04@smu.il.edu
Subject: The Family Business

Greyson, is that weird? Not at all. Isn't diversity a good thing? My dad always says that having diverse interests gives you a leg up in business, so you're already one step ahead of the game. My mom works in the accounts payable department of his office, and my sister is his Field Manager. She never wanted to work for the family but got roped into it two years ago when Dad had a stroke. Sis is Tabitha, and she's pretty fucking cool. A ballbuster, but cool. Do you have any siblings, or are you a lonely only? – Calvin

To: cal.thompson04@smu.il.edu
From: grevkeller0143@state.edu
Subject: Farm Fresh California Milk

Calvin,

Did you think I wouldn't notice you signed that email as Calvin? Cute, cute, cute. Now you're stuck with it ☺ Do I have any siblings? Yes, I have an older brother (Collin, 26) and a younger sister (Reagan, 18). Reagan is a freshman at State with me this year and sometimes stalks me on campus for a free coffee. I work at the Starbucks on campus part-part-time. Don't even ask why they keep me employed, since I'm hardly available to work. Must be my sparkling wit and personality? So, did you at least score any *TRYS* during your game? Grey

To: grevkeller0143@state.edu
From: cal.thompson04@smu.il.edu
Subject: A few more cuts and bruises...

Grey. Holy shit, did you actually google rugby jargon and use TRY in a sentence? Wow, Grey, I have gotta say, I'm actually impressed. And to answer your question—of course I scored a try. They're worth 5 points, and that's where the busted lip came from. Those boys from Ohio are brutes. Changing the subject for a second. So what you're saying is YOUR SISTER STALKS YOU????? At the risk of sounding—oh, I don't know—unsympathetic, can I please point out the fact that perhaps this *stalking* problem RUNS IN YOUR FAMILY???? – Calvin

###

Grey: *I'm sorry, but I can't stop laughing. You can't say funny crap like that during the day. I just choked back a laugh in this class I'm in right now, and the guy in front of me gave me a dirty look.*

Cal: *Fuck that guy AND his dirty look. They can both kiss my ass.*

Grey: *He's trembling at your harsh text.*

Cal: *He would be if I were in that classroom with you.*

Grey: *True. I mean, you with your busted lip and your black eyes and scary glaring. Ten kinds of crazy, remember?*

Cal: *I am pretty scary.*

Grey: *You don't scare ME.*

Cal: *That's because you have a touch of the crazy inside you, too.*

Grey: LOL I DO NOT!!!!!!!!!!!!!!!!!!!

Grey: HE'S LOOKING AT ME AGAIN. *And he is not happy.*

Cal: *Are you wearing a skirt? Maybe he's just trying to see your underwear? In which case, this fake boyfriend WILL come beat his ass.*

Grey: *Okay, now I'm less concerned with my "touch of the crazy" than with your emerging violent streak and wanting to beat people's asses.*

Cal: *Oh, come on. I haven't actually punched anyone in… hours (wink). Fine. It was at last Friday's rugby match, and he deserved it.*

Grey: *Oh lord, Cal…*

Grey: *BTW, no, I'm not wearing a skirt. I'm wearing a dress.*

Cal: *Well, shit.*

Grey: *Is that all you have to say???*

Cal: *No, that's not all I have to say. What else are you wearing?*

Grey: *Oh, heck no, buddy ^^^ I'm not falling for one of those creepy "What are you wearing" sexting messages that lead to no good.*

Cal: *Shhhhhhh. Shush. Just tell me what your dress looks like so I can close my eyes for a second and visualize you sitting in a lecture hall. In a little sundress like the one you were wearing at your house?*

Grey: *Did you seriously SHUSH me via text???*

Cal: *Lol. Shush, woman! I'm not done with my visuals yet.*

Grey: *Wait. You noticed what I was wearing at my house?*

Cal: *Of course I noticed. You're somewhat good-looking.*

Grey: *Cal!!! You brat.*

Cal: *Just stop arguing and send me a selfie.*

Cal: *Please.*

Grey: *Sigh. Fine, here. Since you asked nice.*

Cal: *Shit, wow. I forgot how cute you are.*

Grey: *Cute? Ugh, the kiss of death. Cute is for kittens and grandmas.*

Cal: *Well I can't very well say you look smoke-fucking-hot, can I? That would be weird.*

Cal: *See? That was weird.*

###

To: cal.thompson04@smu.il.edu
From: grevkeller0143@state.edu
Subject: Crappy night

Calvin,

Can I vent to you about my crappy night last night? I don't want to dump on you, but... Sometimes it's hard to talk to my friends about certain things. Sometimes I feel like I'm the only one with problems—well, not really "problems," but I don't think I'm handling the stress of all this responsibility well. Sometimes I wish I... had someone to share it with, you know? Anyway. A group of us went out last night (Wasted Wednesday and all that) to this bar, Major Dingby's. And even though I have a "boyfriend"—go ahead, make fun—all anyone did was try and set me up with people!!!! Pretty sure they're not convinced you're real? Why would they try to SET ME UP when they know—I mean THINK—I have a boyfriend??? It's so disrespectful. How is that for ironic? There was this one guy who wouldn't leave me alone, and all I wanted to do was leave. I also wish I hadn't worn a skirt, because, HELLO, ASS GRABBING. It did nothing but make me feel less… less whole. Less in control. Less special. It's not that I mind being single, but I will admit, when I see other people in happy relationships, I get… Ugh, whatever. So that was my night. And now that I wrote that all out I feel so much better, even if I am being a big baby.

Grey

To: grevkeller0143@state.edu
From: cal.thompson04@smu.il.edu
Subject: RE: Crappy night

Grey. First of all, I hope you didn't just stand there letting some prick cop a feel of your ass. Hearing you talk about it makes me feel shitty and like a dick, because I've groped an ass or two. You're not saying it, but I can hear the frustration in the tone of your message, and on behalf of all douchebags, I apologize for the guy who made you feel violated. Is 'violated' even remotely accurate? – Calvin

###

Grey: *Thank you for that email. It made me feel really, really good.*

Cal: *Really? I'm beginning to wonder if maybe I should double major in counseling.*

Grey: *Calvin, has anyone told you you're a very good listener?*

Cal: *No one—in the history of everybody—has EVER told me I'm a "very good listener." Let's not start any rumors to the contrary.*

Grey: *Well, it's not like you have a choice but to listen when it's just me in an email. I'm sure you would have zoned out if you were sitting across the table from me.*

Cal: *I seriously doubt that.*

###

To: grevkeller0143@state.edu
From: cal.thompson04@smu.il.edu
Subject: Sunday-not-so-Funday

Grey. Feeling any better? I hate weekends. I always feel so fucking restless. Itchy to do something. Just went for a jog, and I think I'm going to take my kayak down to this small lake (that's more of a pond) nearby, blow off some steam. We don't practice on the weekends because sometimes we have matches, so when we don't have anything going on I tend to get cagey. "Calvin has too much energy" is what my teachers used to say. Drove my mom up a wall. I was always up at dawn, rooting through the kitchen in the dark before school, eating everything in sight before taking a run. At least once a week, my parents thought they were being robbed. My mom's grocery bills were ridiculous when I lived at home. Costco has a plaque in my honor from all the pasta my mom used to buy there. So, yeah. On that awkward note—I'm going kayaking. Kind of a bummer that I'm going alone. It's an awesome day out, yeah?

Just thought I'd see how your spirits were. – Calvin

To: cal.thompson04@smu.il.edu
From: grevkeller0143@state.edu
Subject: The countdown continues.

Calvin,

Well, we're less than six weeks from the gala, and tonight we have our sorority meeting. We always have them on Sunday nights. I'll stand and give an update to the entire chapter on the Philanthropy meetings progress, yada, yada, yada… I have a test tomorrow in my Contracts Law class worth half our grade, so before our Chapter meeting—and after—I'll be cramming for that. Spending the day outdoors sounds (long wistful sigh) *divine*. It's so gorgeous outside. Perfect day, and I'm stuck inside ☹ Greyson

###

Cal: *Here's a pic of the lake I'm talking about. Picturesque, hey? See that little island? Sometimes I paddle over and sit on the log hanging over the water. #nofilter*

Grey: *That is STUNNING, Calvin! So jealous.*

Cal: *I'll admit, it is gorgeous, but today for some reason I'm kind of bored. Like I'm missing something.*

Grey: *I wonder what that could be…*

Grey: *Here's a photo of me NOT on the lake* ☹

Cal: *Man, you're pretty.*

Grey: *Here's another one.*

Cal: *Shit, I have to stop texting from this kayak. I just knocked my hat in the water with my paddle because I'm distracted.*

Grey: *Ok. TTYL. Don't fall in!*

###

To: grevkeller0143@state.edu
From: cal.thompson04@smu.il.edu
Subject: Flying solo this weekend definitely sucked.

Morning, Grey. Gotta say, I'm feeling a little guilty I sent you that picture from Lake Holloway yesterday, because you were trapped indoors, but it was so beautiful on the lake. Quiet. There was no one else there except this one couple—they had a tent and were camping on the peninsula of the little island you saw in the picture. Not to be a peeping Tom/creeper/stalker, but I sat and watched them for a little bit before paddling on. Just chilling and lying around in the grass next to their campfire. Looked awesome. It bummed me out though for a second, because it's like you said in one of your emails; I don't mind being single, but seeing that couple made me feel weird. And I'm only telling you this because you're a chick, and I know you have no one to tell—but now I sound like a girl, all whiney and complainey. Haha. – Calvin

To: cal.thompson04@smu.il.edu
From: grevkeller0143@state.edu
Subject: Lurker on the lake.

Cal,

Good morning!!!! Yes, I was jealous that you were out on the lake without me. Maybe someday we could… Um. Yeah. LOL. I actually think it's sweet that you were creeping on those campers. It gives me hope that not all guys are commitment-phobes. YOU'RE not a commitment-phobe, are you, Calvin? Sorry, is that too personal? I don't mean to pry, but now I'm curious. Anyway! Moving on—any big plans for the week…?
Greyson

To: grevkeller0143@state.edu
From: cal.thompson04@smu.il.edu
Subject: Resting up and trying to heal.

Grey. Am I a commitment-phobe? The short answer: no.

Big plans for the week? Not really. Just more of the same shit, different days of the week. Studying, homework, studying, practice, and a match this Friday. It's a home game—our first of the season. Taking advantage of the nice weather, because soon it will get shitty and we'll be playing in snow flurries. Which blows. Speaking of which, my foul language doesn't offend you, does it? I keep forgetting you're classy and not some slutty barfly. – Calvin

To: cal.thompson04@smu.il.edu
From: grevkeller0143@state.edu
Subject: Little Miss not-so-Prim-and-Proper

Calvin,

No, you're swearing doesn't offend me. At all. So no worries. Don't censor yourself around me or you'll exhaust yourself. Besides, clean mouth and proper isn't who you are, and I don't want you to pretend you're something you're not. Who are you playing this Friday? Anyone I would know? Grey

To: grevkeller0143@state.edu
From: cal.thompson04@smu.il.edu
Subject: Assholes and away games

Grey, we're playing a little school called Notre Dame. Ever heard of them? ;) It's a home game, and thank God they're coming to us. I hate being stuck for hours on a bus, even if they're charter with DVD players and shit. You have no idea what these rugby guys are like, myself included. LOL. Bunch of loudmouth assholes. Don't know how we've never been blacklisted by the bus company. I guess there's always still a chance. Glad I can say shit like shit around you and that you're not easily insulted. Gotta say though, if I watched my mouth for anyone, it would probably be you. But maybe that's just the lack of sleep talking. - Calvin

###

Grey: *Saw the date stamp on your email last night. What were you doing up so late???*

Cal: *Studying. We must have some of the same classes because it's Contracts Law. Actually really love it.*

Grey: *Me too. I wonder sometimes if I should be pre-law LOL.*

Cal: *I don't know. I think you're probably too soft to be a lawyer.*

Grey: *What's THAT supposed to mean??*

Cal: *You don't have the killer instinct. I could tell when you were all 'sorry this' and 'sorry that' when I came to kick Greyson's ass. You should have stood up to me.*

Grey: *And said what? What I did was wrong!*

Cal: *Yeah, but still. Most girls would have at least screamed and yelled at me for showing up on their doorstep.*

Grey: *Well then, I guess I'm not like most girls.*

Cal: *Yeah, I'm beginning to see that.*

###

To: grevkeller0143@state.edu
From: cal.thompson04@smu.il.edu
Subject: Dentist on call

Greyson. Okay, this week is already going to shit. We had practice today, and I almost got a tooth knocked out. Remember the guy I had with me at your house in the red shirt? His name is Aaron, but for all practical purposes, we'll call him Shitbag. Moron fucking knocked me in the mouth when I wasn't wearing a mouth guard, which was a stupid thing for me to forget. Definitely chipped my tooth, blood everywhere. Emergency visit to the dentist. And let's just put it this way: it's a good thing I'm only your fake boyfriend, because you wouldn't want to kiss this mouth. – Cal

To: cal.thompson04@smu.il.edu
From: grevkeller0143@state.edu
Subject: Face plant.

Calvin,

Does it hurt? I've only been nailed in the mouth once, and it was by my brother when I was 12. Which would have made him 19. We were playing football in the backyard with some of his friends when he came home from college for Easter, and he lobbed the ball right at my face. A spiral toss, full force. Nothing was knocked out but me. Laid me flat out. Fat, bloody lip for almost two weeks. My parents were so pissed. I still refuse to toss the ball around with him LOL. He'll never live it down. Speaking of bloody lips, who's to say no one would want to kiss you? I bet SOME girls get turned on by beat-up-looking athletes. Do you still have that black eye? That's bonus points. Brings your average up considerably, and I definitely find that sexy. Grey

###

Cal: *My face still hurts.*
Grey: *Rub some dirt on it.*
Cal: *I don't have any. I live in a concrete jungle.*
Grey: *Poor baby.*
Cal: *>tear<*
Grey: LOLOL

###

To: cal.thompson04@smu.il.edu
From: greykeller0143@state.edu
Subject: Nurse Greyson Keller at your service…
Calvin,

How's our patient today? The lip and teeth any better? I hope Aaron hasn't mysteriously disappeared,

because that would make me an accessory to a crime. And then I would have to report you to the authorities.
Grey

To: grevkeller0143@state.edu
From: cal.thompson04@smu.il.edu
Subject: Naughty Nurse Keller? Yes please.

Grey. Wow, you would make the world's shittiest nurse. I'm sensing all your sympathy lies with Aaron, and I won't stand for it. We're not supposed to rough each other up in practice. I swear to fucking God he's pissed that I haven't gotten Melody's number for him. I don't know where he thinks I'd GET it from, because I haven't told anyone you and I have been talking. – Calvin

###

Grey: *So now I'm your dirty little secret?*
Cal: *No, that's not what I meant at all. You're more like…*
Grey: *More like…? Come on, tell me. Don't be shy.*
Cal: *Me, shy? Yeah, right.*
Grey: *Don't change the subject. If I'm not your dirty little secret, then what am I?*
Cal: *You're more like—this is going to sound really fucking dumb.*

Grey: *SAY IT OR I SWEAR TO GOD CALVIN I WILL COME FIND YOU.*

Cal: *Well, in that case I'm going to zip my lips shut.*

Grey: *Aww, you are so cute.*

Cal: *You're not my dirty little secret. You're my guilty pleasure.*

Cal: *Oh my god, that did sound fucking dumb.*

Grey: *Hold on. I'm going to pass out now from shock. That wasn't dumb—it was the sweetest thing I've ever heard.*

Cal: *And THAT'S ^^^ the reason I shouldn't have said anything.*

Grey: *I'm taking a screenshot of that and saving it for eternity so I can stare at it at night when I'm alone.*

Cal: *Wow. Spoken like a true stalker.*

Grey: *LOL.*

###

To: grevkeller0143@state.edu
From: cal.thompson04@smu.il.edu

Subject: Worse than a bunch of women. No offense.

Greyson. My roommates are driving me fucking crazy. If they don't stop asking about you, I'm moving out. Mason checks his *Twatter* constantly, looking for my name in your feed, and mopes around like a sad puppy dog when he can't find one. It's annoying. Could you do me a favor and get him off my back by throwing the dog a small bone? – Calvin

###

@Grey_VKeller Tweeted: *The countdown to Gala continues. Thanks 4 dinner last night @calthompson3192 the poem & wine & roses & chocolates were 2 MUCH! Kisses to my big SWEETIE POOH #bestboyfriend*

###

Cal: *I hate you so hard right now.*

Grey: **blank stare* Was it something I said?? I tried to use every available character #140*

Cal: *That was really fucking rude. They are RIDING MY ASS right now. Calling me pussy whipped. Hope you're happy, you brat.*

Grey: *Oh, don't be a baby. You asked me to send the tweet.*

Cal: *You know damn well that's not what I meant. Who's moving out of state and changing their name? >> This guy <<*

Grey: *Changing your name? *claps happily* Ooh, ooh! Let me help you pick one!!!! What about Chet Montgomery? That sounds sporty and badass.*

Cal: *No.*

Grey: *Allan Thouroughgood*

Cal: *Oh my god.*

Grey: *Randolph Christian Kuttnauer*

Cal: *WHERE the HELL are you coming up with these?*

Grey: *Those don't sound regal to you? Or manly?*

Cal: *No.*

Grey: *I've got it!!! Dark Gray Keller.*

Cal: *LOLOL Okay. I'll admit, that one was funny.*

Grey: *☺ I try. TRY. GET IT? GET IT???*

Cal: *Honestly, Grey. What am I going to do with you…*

Grey: *I might have some suggestions.*

Cal: *No comment.*

###

To: cal.thompson04@smu.il.edu
From: grevkeller0143@state.edu
Subject: We're becoming THAT couple ;) haha

Calvin,

You're not still mad about the tweet, are you? Believe me—I got as much shit from my friends as you probably did. Apparently, when you publically call someone Sweetie Pooh, it makes people want to toss their cookies inside their preppy monogram tote bags. Or so I've been told. Multiple times. Jemma, your roommate's cousin, has been getting the scoop on you from Mason, and now she wants me to stay away from you. Says you're only going to break my heart because you don't "do" relationships. Oh, and you're a total dickhead. (Mason's words, not mine). Oddly enough, I ended up defending you like this charade is real. What's THAT all about?! Grey

To: grevkeller0143@state.edu
From: cal.thompson04@smu.il.edu
Subject: Admit it. I'm growing on you.

Greyson. No, I'm not still mad. Actually, I wasn't mad to begin with, just surprised. Want to know the truth? I don't actually mind the teasing. What's THAT all about? – Calvin

To: cal.thompson04@smu.il.edu
From: grevkeller0143@state.edu
Subject: Bats in the Belfry

Dear Calvin,

Do you realize we've been emailing and texting for over three weeks now? Every time I giggle at my phone—at something YOU said—my roommates and sisters give me the weirdest looks. At this point there is no doubt they think you're real. It's going to make things that much more awkward when Gala night arrives. I cannot wait for this thing to be over. Which reminds me, pretty soon I'm going to have to publicly break up with you. Don't worry, it will be mutual, even though having a real life boyfriend would have been handy last night. We had a BAT in our house. I swear to God, Calvin, the screaming coming from Melody… My eardrums shattered. WHAT? *Did you say something?* I CAN'T HEAR YOU! We must have called our landlord five times, and he never showed up. Finally, Beth, my other roommate, called one of the guys from our brother fraternity, and not one but THREE of them showed up—three of us, three of them. See how they planned that?—with tennis rackets, of course, like THAT was a smart idea. One of the brothers kept asking all these questions about you. His name is Dylan, and if he touched my leg once he touched it six times while grilling me about you. Or the Cal I made up. Anyway, he kept telling me about how long-distance relationships never work. I wanted to smack him. Grey. PS: The bat is gone. FOR NOW.

To: grevkeller0143@state.edu
From: cal.thompson04@smu.il.edu
Subject: RE: Bats in the Belfry

WHAT THE FUCK, GREYSON? I don't even know where to start. How does a fake boyfriend respond to an email like that? I can't come pound some dude's face in because he touched you just like I can't beat your landlord's ass for not showing up to kill a bat—and that infuriates me. I'm going to take a deep breath here and calm the fuck down for a second. – Calvin

To: cal.thompson04@smu.il.edu
From: grevkeller0143@state.edu
Subject: There's only room for ONE (fake) boyfriend in my life.

Cal,

I'm sorry I upset you. It really wasn't that big of a deal. I mean, yes, Dylan kind of upset me, but he wasn't doing it intentionally. Well… okay. That's a lie because he was obviously hitting on me pretty hard and CLEARLY trying to badmouth you. Or the *OTHER* Cal. LOL. It makes me—I don't know—happy that you care enough to get mad. Who knew that we would become FRIENDS? Life is crazy, isn't it? Just in the middle of cooking dinner here, but I wanted to send you a quick note. What time is your match tomorrow? Grey.

To: grevkeller0143@state.edu
From: cal.thompson04@smu.il.edu
Subject: Wasted man meat.

Grey. What did you end up making for dinner? I bet it was better than what we had—or didn't have. We bought a few choice steak filets that Mason immediately burned the CRAP out of on the grill. Charred. Fifty bucks flushed down the shitter, and he kept blaming the charcoal. Our game tomorrow starts at 6pm, and it's 80 minutes—two 40-minute halves, obviously. Have you ever been to one? This match is going to set the tone for our entire season. Aaron has his sights set on a professional team in Ireland after graduation and has a good chance at being signed. We've been friends since middle school, so his level of play is surreal, even for me. I love the kid like a brother and I'm really proud of him. I swear to God, Grey, if you ever repeat that… - Cal

To: cal.thompson04@smu.il.edu
From: grevkeller0143@state.edu
Subject: Sisterhoods and Bromances

Calvin,

Who would I even TELL about your love for Aaron? My sorority sisters? The Twitterverse? Anyway, I don't get why guys never want to talk about their feelings for each other. It's really stupid if you ask me. A slap on the ass among men during a sporting event hardly a brotherhood makes. Wait. Did that even make sense??? Whatever, I'm not deleting it. Haha. You probably won't even see this because you're getting ready to rugby. Grey

###

Cal: *Oh, I saw it.*

Grey: *You're there!!*

Cal: *Grey, it's only noon. Lol. Where else would I be?*

Cal: *And for your information, rugby players do* NOT *slap each other on the ass. Ever. I'd get punched in the face if I ever swatted another dude in the ass.*

Grey: *Want to test that theory? Swat someone on the ass and see what happens…*

Cal: *No.*

Grey: *Boo, hiss.*

Cal: *So. Got anything going on tomorrow afternoon?*

Grey: *Maybe. I don't have afternoon classes on Fridays, so the girls and I might take a short trip.*

Cal: *That sounds… terrible.*

Grey: *That's 'cause you're a party pooper.*

Grey: *Incidentally, if you had a drink of choice after your game, what would it be?*

Cal: *Um…??? That's really random.*

Grey: *Humor me.*

Cal: *Probably a green tea lemonade.*

Grey: *Ah, a Starbucks man.*

Cal: *GTG. Team meeting in twenty.*

Grey: ☺

chapter four

Calvin

I'm pulling the slobbery mouth guard off my teeth when I see her.

I briskly shake my head side to side, beads of perspiration flying out of my damp hair, and squint up into the stands, convinced my eyes are playing tricks on me.

Under the stadium light, among the SMU and Notre Dame fans donning their navy and gold school colors, Grey stands, her long blonde hair whipping in the wind as she makes her way, one metal bleacher step at a time, down towards the rugby field.

I shake my head again. Holy fuck. What is she *doing* here?

My breath catches as I blink in her direction—not just from being winded from the hard-fought game we just won. No. I'm suddenly winded from an adrenaline rush of another kind: Lust. Anticipation. Uncertainty.

I stand frozen on the sidelines, surrounded by my teammates packing up their gear. Another bead of sweat rolls down my neck and drips onto my already soaked jersey.

"Hottie approaching at three o'clock," the team's athletic trainer, Paul, announces. "Wow. She's... wow. "

"That's no ordinary hottie, Paul," Mason announces, slapping a hand down on my shoulder. "That's Tighthead's stalker. Steer clear."

Paul stares, captivated, at Greyson's encroaching figure. "Why would anyone want to steer clear of *that*?" Lucky for Paul, he just sounds fascinated, not perverted.

Aaron stuffs a towel and sweatshirt into his duffel before joining in the mocking. "Holy shit, man. It looks like your stalker really *is* a stalker! Were you full of shit when you said she wasn't stalking you?"

"Are you guys being serious?" Paul, armed with this new information, tilts his head and appraises her. "*She's* a stalker? No way."

"Stop being an asshole, Mason. And stop fucking using that word," I growl, shoving him out of my personal space. Grey's throng of friends lingers behind her, obediently up in the bleachers as she approaches me, her bright white smile lighting her stunning face.

A low whistle of appreciation escapes Paul's lips. "Damn, Tighthead, *that* girl is into *you*? No offense."

Shit. Fuck.

"She is way out of your league, bro," Mason charitably points out.

Don't I know it.

She's gorgeous, and I'm a mutt, and Mason's reminder pisses me off.

"Would you all just effing go away," I demand with another shove, and he laughs, giving Grey a little wave before hefting his equipment bag over his shoulder and retreating towards the university's field house.

"Come on, guys. Let's give Tighthead and his girlfriend here some *pri-va-cy*." The way he says it has everyone, including our coach, snickering.

"Fuck off, all of you," I sneer, embarrassed and irritated. Several of the guys are avidly checking out Greyson, and that's pissing me off too.

"Tsk, tsk. That's not a very nice way to talk to your friends," Grey calls out to me, and I hear several of my teammates laughing in the distance as Grey steps onto the playing field in those same wedge sandals she wore the day we met, her dark jean capris hugging her long legs. And are my eyes deceiving me, or is she eyeing me up with unconcealed appreciation?

"I didn't see you smacking anyone's ass during the match," she teases. "That's a tad disappointing. I thought maybe you were lying when you said you never did that." Her eyes roam to Mason, who keeps glancing back at us as he trudges to the building.

Greyson's keen eyes notice. "What'd he do to piss you off?"

She's thirty feet away.

I swallow the hard lump in my throat. "He was being an ass."

Fifteen.

"Well, never mind him."

Five feet.

She extends her hand, presenting me with a large green tea lemonade from Starbucks. "The ice melted because I couldn't give it to you sooner. Sorry." Perspiration slides off the plastic cup.

Shell shocked, I take it from her while she continues gushing.

"My gosh, Cal," she breathes when she's standing in front of me, her hands reaching up to hover over my hardened pecs like she's about to run them up-and-down my broad chest.

I hold my breath, but she drops them back to her side.

But then…

"You are amazing! You look so *incredible* out there, Cal. I swear, I couldn't take my eyes off you." Moving in closer, she actually goes up on her tiptoes and plants a kiss on my sweat-drenched cheek. As if she couldn't stop herself.

I watch, transfixed, when Grey licks her lips instead of wiping the sweat on her mouth off with her hand. "Wow, you smell good. Like a man."

Jesus H *Christ*.

"Um, hi?" I manage, fighting the urge to blurt out, *What the hell are you doing here?*

"Surprise!" Grey giggles, a delighted little twinkle that tinges the apples of her cheeks a pretty pink color. "I couldn't stay away. The temptation to show up unexpectedly was impossible to resist." She gives me a wink and shoves my bicep, her fingers sinking into my skin and lingering far too long to be accidental.

She prattles on. "Well, I mean I *could* have stayed away—but I didn't want to."

Down in my spandex rugby pants is the telltale twitching of an impending hard-on.

Fuck.

"Grey, uh…" I tip my head to our audience. My teammates are huddled on the far side of the field, avidly watching with interest, while her sorority sisters do the same from up in the bleachers.

She glances back over her shoulder and shrugs without a care. "My friends wanted to come down here, but of course I wouldn't let them. You're safe from the inquisition, if that's what you're worried about." Grey runs a hand through her highlighted wavy hair and gives it a shake.

It settles on her shoulder like a silky cloud, shining under the stadium lights like a halo.

Mesmerized, I stare down into her large, laughing hazel eyes, darkened with black eyeliner and coated with a heavy layer of mascara. She's wearing a simple white t-shirt, but it's tight, and my eyes are drawn to the smooth bronze skin in the deep V neck.

Her brown eyebrows are raised at me expectantly.

Oh shit. She wants me to say something.

"Hmm." Her hands settle on her narrow hips. "You were much chattier when you came to my house. Is everything okay?"

"Yeah, I'm just—you want the truth?"

"No, I want you to lie." Grey rolls those brilliant eyes with a smile. "Yes, of course I want the truth."

"I'm shocked to see you. It's one thing for me to ambush *you*, but another for you to ambush *me*."

"Well, if it makes you feel better, we can't stay long. I have to get that crew of misfit toys behind me back to campus. A few of them are running a 5k tomorrow, and they want to stuff themselves with pasta." She rolls her eyes again. "They think they're pro athletes now and want to carb load. By the way, this is one of those 5ks where you wear a fluffy tutu and get pelted with color bombs, so…"

Again with the raised eyebrow.

I can't stand it. "I know I'm being fucking awkward, okay? Just say it."

"You're a *little* awkward." She crosses her arms and taps her foot. "But I find you *very* charming."

"Stop looking at me like that," I mumble.

"How am I looking at you? I'm not doing anything." Greyson laughs. "I'm standing here *talking*."

She playfully gives my tricep another tap, the contact from her feather-light touch giving me goosebumps *and* a goddamn boner.

The tightening in my shorts has my jaw clenching and my nostrils flare. "Stop flirting."

"Why?"

Fuck it. "Because it's making me hard."

Instead of being offended by the lewd comment, Greys hazel eyes leisurely skim down my body to my spandex shorts, alive with interest. The air between us crackles and sizzles.

"Spoilsport," she whispers, the disappointment in her voice palpable.

At that moment, I'm certain of one thing: this girl is going to be the death of me.

She tips her chin thoughtfully at me when I frown. "Okay, okay. I'll leave. Tell Mason and Aaron your *stalker* says hi."

"You heard that?"

"Um, yeah—they were practically shouting."

"Sorry."

"Do I look like I care?" She flips her hair and shoots a flirty smile over to my group of teammates, wiggling her fingers in their direction. They stare back at the pretty girl, transfixed, before several meaty arms enthusiastically wave back. "Could they be any more obvious?" Greyson's laugh fills the night air. "They're nosier than a group of sorority girls. Look at them pretending to be busy instead of heading into the building."

"They're just staring because you're kind of nice looking." I sound disgruntled.

"Nice looking?" Grey laughs again and reaches up to touch my jaw, running a thumb along my busted up lip. "Aww, see? You can be sweet."

"Yeah, whatever." A smile curls my lips.

"Alright, well. I'm going to go now." She lets out a little puff of air and closes the space between us. "Can you do me a small favor, since my friends are watching?"

"That depends." I cross my arms, one hand fisting the Starbucks, noting with satisfaction that my biceps are bulging nicely. "What is it?"

Grey notices too.

"See, remember how I told you no one knows I made you up? Well, it wouldn't seem *natural* for me to just walk away right now. You know, without…" Her sentence trails off, and she stares me down.

I'm not following. "Without *what?*"

"A good-bye kiss, you idiot."

It takes me a few to realize she's being serious. She *actually* wants me to kiss her. This gorgeous, smart, funny girl wants *me* to kiss *her*.

"You're asking me to kiss you." It's a statement, not a question. "I have stitches in my lip."

"Do the stitches bother you? It doesn't have to be real—just one for show. If you can stand to put your lips near me."

Now it's my turn to roll my eyes. "Don't be so dramatic. I think I can manage."

Her eyes shine. "Put the cup down."

The air crackles around us like unharnessed electricity. Bending slowly, I do as I'm told, setting the green tea lemonade on the playing field.

"Well? Get closer, you shameless hussy. Unless you're afraid to get dirty."

"I'm not afraid to get dirty if you're not."

"Would you stop saying shit like that? Jesus." I grasp her arm, tugging her into my damp, mud-stained rugby jersey, trailing my calloused hands up her smooth arms. Grey sighs and leans into me, returning the favor. The tips of her fingers start at my wrists, tracing their way up the sensitive skin of my underarms. She flattens her palms and closes them around the corded muscles of my flexed biceps.

Her breasts press against my sweat-soaked chest.

My cock gets harder, and any intentions of a chaste good-bye kiss go up in smoke as my hormones rage inside me like a wildfire.

I gently cup her neck in my large palms, kneading the nape and cradling her jaw when her head lists to one side with a moan.

My fingers find themselves threaded through her thick, silk-spun hair.

Bodies drawn together as if by necessity, our hot lips press together, softly at first. Tentatively. I hesitate a few seconds, inhaling to harness my raging testosterone levels, and begin pulling away.

"Wait." Grey's delicate hands gently glide up my biceps to my shoulders, her index finger tracing my square jawline, then the lobe of an ear. "Don't back away yet. Please."

Without thinking, I grab her wrist and roll my head, bringing her palm to my mouth and planting a wet kiss there. I kiss the tips of her fingers and her palm, running my nose along the velvety skin of her wrist and inhaling the musky smell of her perfume.

Her lips part as she watches me, her pupils dilated.

"God, Grey."

Our foreheads touch. The tips of our noses follow.

A few millimeters closer and our lips part. Mouths touch. Tongues meet.

"Kiss me, Cal," Grey begs against my mouth, her voice a whisper in the breeze. "*Kiss* me."

Fuck it. I'm going all in.

I snake my arms around her waist and haul her in, so flush with her body that I'm cradled in between her legs. I groan. She moans, and her hands travel south, down over my firm ass, squeezing it through my thin shorts.

Holy shit, *yes*.

I lose half my brain cells in that moment—then the rest—when she sucks my tongue farther into her mouth, like she's actually enjoying herself. Her tongue darts out, licking along the deep cut on my lip.

I give her a few more kisses before I tighten my grip on her arms and, regretfully, give her a small push to create some space between us.

"Shit, Grey, we have to stop." My breathing is labored, but so is hers. "Jesus. This is nuts."

"I don't want to," she pouts against my lips.

"I don't either, but my dick is hard as a rock and I'm wearing fucking spandex. People are watching."

As if on cue, my teammates begin cat-calling from the field house. Assholes.

She huffs; it's adorable. "Okay, fine. But only because I don't want to be called any more nasty names 'cause I can't keep my hands to myself."

"Trust me, it's no hardship," I feebly joke, my voice catching when Grey runs her palms up the front of my jersey, tracing the outline of the team name screen printed there. I reach my hand between our bodies, adjusting my groin and jockstrap before capturing her hands to hold them still. "I'm going to be walking crooked for a week."

Grey takes a step back, giving me a once-over and pausing on the bulge in my shorts before averting her eyes and glancing up into the bleachers as her hands fall to her sides. She swallows hard and clears her throat. "You played great tonight, Cal. I'm proud of you."

"Grey, why…"

"Yes?"

"…are you here?"

We stare at one another, and I know by the expression on her face that she's doing what I'm doing: memorizing every line in my face, every curve of my body.

Just in case we… just in case this is the last time.

And there goes that crack and sizzle.

Grey closes the gap between us. Slowly, her soft lips press against my mouth, tenderly resting there. "You know why I'm here, Cal Thompson."

She turns reluctantly, glancing back at me at least a half dozen times as I watch her go.

I don't how long I stood there.

#

Cal: *I'm sorry I manhandled you tonight.*

Grey: *If I remember correctly, I did basically TELL you to kiss me, so in a way, I was doing the manhandling. For the sake of my friends, of course. And my charade.*

Cal: *Of course.*

Grey: *For the sake of science?*

Cal: *That sounds even less plausible.*

Grey: *Fine, don't believe me.*

Cal: *Fine, I won't.*

#

@Grey_VKeller Tweeted: *@tightheadthompson you sexy sexy beast*

#

Cal: *I know you did NOT just tweet that shit.*

Grey: *Are getting teased again by your friends? Come on, it can't be that bad.*

Cal: *Is this all just a joke to you? A sorority prank?*

Grey: *Is WHAT a joke???*

Cal: *Sexy sexy beast? Seriously, WHAT THE FUCK, GREYSON?*

Grey: *WHY ARE YOU SO PISSED OFF?! CALM DOWN*

Cal: *You can't say shit like that. It makes you sound like a goddamn…*

Grey: *A goddamn WHAT*

Cal: *Forget it. Just don't say shit like that.*

Grey: *I will NOT forget it. Tell me what your freaking problem is.*

Grey: *And for the record, you overreacting jackass, I MEANT IT.*

Cal: *Oh.*

Grey: *Oh?*

Grey: *Hello? You there?*

Grey: *Cal?*

Grey: *Okay then.*

chapter five

Greyson

"I don't understand. You tweeted that he was a sexy beast, and then he goes radio silence on you? That's so messed up."

I drum a number 2 pencil on the wooden table, and blow a puff of air at my bangs to move them out of my eyes. "I guess I don't get it. I thought that maybe, when he kissed me, we were… I don't know."

"Becoming more than pen pals?"

"Yes. Because I felt that kiss *everywhere*, Mel. Everywhere. That wasn't a kiss between two friends."

Melody speaks slowly then, choosing her words carefully. "I mean, I know it's a weird thing to ask, but do you think you scared him away?"

I give her a hard look. "What's that supposed to mean?"

"Nothing! I just wonder if he thought maybe you were... making fun of him? Lying?"

I ignore that she just called me a liar, but my mouth still gapes in indignation. "Making *fun* of him? Why would you even *say* that?"

"Well, jeez, Grey. Look at him. He isn't winning any beauty contests."

My mouth falls open even wider, and the rash on my chest shoots up my neck at a breakneck pace, coloring my cheeks, nose, and forehead. My face is flaming hot, which I bet it looks spectacular against my light blonde hair. "Melody! What the *hell*. I think he's gorgeous!"

"Well, yeah—*you* do. But you didn't think he was so hot when he showed up at the house. You think he's hot because you're finally getting to know him. That's why you think he's attractive; he's grown on you. Everyone else, erm, not so much."

"You—that's so mean." I stand abruptly, knocking a cup of pens over with a curse. Tears threaten to spill out of the corners of my eyes. I wipe them away angrily. "Not all of us just want to date pretty frat boys."

Melody sighs, her eyes pleading with me. "I'm sorry. That's not... this is coming out all wrong."

My bottom lip trembles.

"Grey." Melody stands. "You're beautiful. And sweet. And funny. Of course everyone expects you to hook up with some GQ model. Not some... Not a busted-up *rugby* player from SMU. I'm just trying to be honest."

"I do *not* like you right now."

"Grey, you don't even know this guy."

"Yes I do." I cross my arms and stare out the window into the yard, tuning her out. Softly, I whisper, "I know enough."

###

To: cal.thompson04@smu.il.edu
From: grevkeller0143@state.edu
Subject: Please talk to me.

Calvin,

It's been two days. Why are you shutting me out? I don't understand. I don't understand why you over reacted to the tweet, but I'm sorry if I embarrassed you in front of your friends. I called you sexy and I meant it. I wasn't making fun of you—how could you THINK that??? I thought we were becoming friends. I miss you. I miss my friend. Grey

To: grevkeller0143@state.edu
From: cal.thompson04@smu.il.edu
Subject: I'm an ass.

You're right. I overreacted. I don't know how to explain it without sounding like a complete douchenozzle, so can we just forget about it? I feel like a tool. And since we're friends and I'm being honest, this is exactly how I would treat you if you were a dude. I'd give you the silent treatment until I got over myself. So you should feel pretty good about that. – Cal

To: cal.thompson04@smu.il.edu
From: grevkeller0143@state.edu
Subject: Best Friends 4Eva

Cal,

Yes, I'll forget about it, but… You know what, never mind—I'm just so relieved you emailed me back. I'll keep this light hearted. After all, we hardly know each other. As for you treating me like one of your guy friends, well—I'm flattered. Kind of? Have you ever had a girl that's a friend before? The distance between us certainly makes it easier to have that kind of relationship, yeah? I doubt I could manage to be *friends* friends if we were at the same school—if we were in the same town. Grey

To: grevkeller0143@state.edu
From: cal.thompson04@smu.il.edu
Subject: Huh?

Greyson, I'm not even sure what that's supposed to mean.

To: cal.thompson04@smu.il.edu
From: grevkeller0143@state.edu
Subject: Seriously?

Read between the lines, Calvin. And why are you emailing me this? Wouldn't it be easier to text? Grey.

To: grevkeller0143@state.edu
From: cal.thompson04@smu.il.edu
Subject: Still don't have a clue. Sorry.

Grey. I'm not texting because I had already composed the email. And last time I checked, I was a guy—and one that gets concussions on a regular basis. You need to spell it out for me. – Cal

To: cal.thompson04@smu.il.edu
From: grevkeller0143@state.edu
Subject: Forget I said anything.

Cal,

I'm not in the mood to explain myself. Maybe some other time.

###

Cal: *This is going to get ridiculous if we don't talk.*
Grey: *What's going to get ridiculous?*

Cal: *You know what? Never mind. I'm not playing games with you.*

Grey: *Time. Out. Why are you being so stubborn about this? I don't know what flipped your switch, but you need to explain it. Answer me, Calvin.*

Cal: *You're right. I'm sorry. You're my friend, and it was an asshole thing to do, and I'm sorry.*

Grey: *I like you, Calvin. I think you're sexy and handsome and funny. Accept it and move on. And stop being an ass.*

Cal: *Have you always been this bossy?*

Grey: *Yes.*

Cal: *I like it.*

Grey: *I know you do. Why do you think I'm acting so bossy?*

###

To: greykeller0143@state.edu
From: cal.thompson04@smu.il.edu
Subject: Not that kind of trim work

Greyson. Going home this weekend to help my dad do some landscaping. My mom gets all weird about having all the shrubs and flower beds weeded and cut down before it gets cold out, so… just wanted to let you know. My folks get pissed when I'm constantly checking my phone. Disrespectful and all that shit. – Cal

To: cal.thompson04@smu.il.edu
From: grevkeller0143@state.edu
Subject: TWO WHOLE DAYS?

Calvin,

So what you're saying is, you don't want me to feel bad when you're MIA for a few days? Aww, that's sweet. Very considerate to let me know. I will admit that I have gotten used to talking with you during the day. Well, not "talking," but you get my point. Does your sister have to partake in this landscaping torture, too? Grey

To: grevkeller0143@state.edu
From: cal.thompson04@smu.il.edu
Subject: Evil Mastermind

Grey. Yes, everyone will be there. My parents are Equal Opportunity Sadists. But Tabby (aka: the smart one in this case) will throw a fit at some point and pick a fight so my mom yells and kicks her out of the yard. IT'S SO UNFAIR. She's a genius. – Cal

To: cal.thompson04@smu.il.edu
From: grevkeller0143@state.edu
Subject: Why should Tabitha have all the fun?

Calvin,

Maybe you should beat her to it. Where are you from originally, anyway? I don't think we've ever talked about it. My parents moved this summer from Lake

Walton to another little lake community just south called Six Rivers. It's also a resort town, but there's tons to do there, which is a nice change. Lake Walton was pretty small—the closest Target was a day trip. Grey

###

Cal: *You did NOT say Six Rivers.*

Grey: *Yes, why?*

Cal: *Take a wild guess.*

Grey: *SHUT UP. No way.*

Cal: *Yes way. Well, next town over. 20 minutes on a bad day.*

Grey: *There is NO WAY you live near where I live.*

Grey: *You know what this means, don't you?!*

Cal: *That we can be best friends and do karate in the garage?*

Grey: **crickets* That made absolutely no sense.*

Cal: *Never mind. It's from a movie. LOL. Tell me what you were going to say before when you said, "You know what this means, don't you?" and I so rudely made a movie reference.*

Grey: *Well, besides you being hopelessly clueless, this means we can be buddies during summer and the holidays and hang out! We can have drinks at that bar near the lake.*

Cal: *Sully's on the Lake? It's not near the lake, it's ON the lake. LOL*

Grey: *See. This is why we need to hang out when we're home.*

Cal: *What are the odds?*

Grey: *It's fate.*

Cal: *Oh…. boy.*

Grey: *You can show me the sights. We can float on the lake.*

Cal: *Did you say FLOAT on the lake?*

Grey: *Yeah, you know, on rafts?*

Cal: *Ah, okay. So, literally floating. Will this floating require bathing suits?*

Grey: *Not necessarily.*

Cal: *Are you flirting with me?*

Grey: *I think it's really sad you can't tell when a girl is flirting with you. But since you asked, I wouldn't dare. Remember the last time I tried that? #epicfail #sexybeast #angrycalvin*

Cal: *Fine. But in my defense, no one has ever called me sexy. I thought you were being a bitch.*

Grey: *You are LYING. How is that possible?*

Cal: *Which part? The sexy part or the bitch part?*

Grey: *You are getting sexier and sexier by the day. Sorry, but it's true. Time to accept the facts.*

chapter six

To: grevkeller0143@state.edu
From: cal.thompson04@smu.il.edu
Subject: Warning! Warning!

Grey. As I suspected, my mom drove us nuts over the weekend with her demands. The woman is obsessed with mulching. And, as I predicted, Tabby picked a fight and Mom kicked her out of the yard. The brat winked at me as she fake stormed off. I can't freaking believe my mom still falls for that bullshit. The good news is, all I had to do was drive the bobcat while my dad raked leaves into the shovel. What can I say about Sunday? For starters, my damn sister tricked me into telling her about you. I don't know how she figured it out, but I must have been checking my phone about a hundred times—just in case you decided to send a message—and she caught me. When she tried stealing my phone and I pitched a bitch fit instead of letting her take it, she knew there was shit on here I didn't want her to see. Boy, was she a pain in my ass. The entire day she tried to steal my phone. Wanting to see pictures of you. Asking a shit ton of annoying questions. If you get a friend request from

Tabitha Thompson, would you do me a huge favor and DELETE IT?

What did you do this weekend? – Cal

To: cal.thompson04@smu.il.edu
From: grevkeller0143@state.edu
Subject: I consider creeping research.

Calvin,

In fact, I DID get a friend request from a Tabitha Thompson! LOL. No worries, I haven't decided what to do about it yet. I did sneak onto her page, though. She looks awesome. Very beautiful. My objective, of course, was to find pictures of you. Très stalkerish of me, wouldn't you say? Whatever. I got all giddy and girly over a few—the one of you in a tux for your senior prom? OMG. So handsome. And the one of you with your childhood dog? Must say, Calvin, I have something of a crush on you. I can admit that, right, now that we're pen pals? Grey

To: grevkeller0143@state.edu
From: cal.thompson04@smu.il.edu
Subject: Creeping, lurking = Same thing

Grey. Not surprised that you were lurking on my sister's pics. That picture of me with the dog? Brownie, his name was—he was the shit. Cried like a baby when my parents put him to sleep. I don't even want to know if you saw the picture of me snuggling Sparkles, the kitty cat I had when I was 3. Tabby posted that one last year for my birthday, that rude bitch. Shit. That was a joke. I would never call her that to her face; she'd scratch my eyes out. My sister, not the cat. – Cal

###

Cal: *By the way, I've decided I will allow you to have a crush on me.*

Grey: *How magnanimous of you.*

Cal: *You're welcome.*

Grey: *You ass.*

Cal: *Speaking of asses, yours is incredible.*

Grey: *Well, aren't you just full of compliments today! I've got one for you: I could stare at your firm, tight ass in those rugby spandex all day long.*

Cal: *Holy shit, that is NOT what I was expecting you to say.*

Grey: *Why?*

Cal: *Because you're classy.*

Grey: *Maybe, but I also have eyes. And hormones. I can't say you have a firm, tight ass? Okay, fine. Can we at least talk about your buff arms? DROOL.*

Cal: *NO! Maybe. Okay, fine.*

Grey: **pouting* I want to talk about your tattoos.*

Cal: *Thank god you're an hour away, because I can't spend the whole night jerking off—*

Cal: *Shit, I did NOT mean to send that.*

Cal: *Ugh. It didn't even make any sense.*

Cal: *Greyson, fucking say something!*

Grey: *Shush. Shhhh. Shhh. I'm not done visualizing you doing naughty, naughty things to yourself *closes eyes* Also, why did you TYPE it if you didn't mean to send it? WHAT THE HELL?? LOLOLOL*

Grey: *The WHOLE night jerking off? Wow. That's some stamina you must have…*

Cal: *Oh my god. This is my worst nightmare*

Grey: *^^^ you sound like such a girl.*

Cal: *Wait. Did you just screenshot that shit????*

Grey: *No. Maybe. Okay, fine. Yes.*

###

Cal: *What are you up to right now?*

Grey: *I'm about to walk into work. But instead I'm sitting here in a chair by the door like a creeper, texting you.*

Cal: *Sorry.*

Grey: *Don't APOLOGIZE. Sheesh, Calvin. How could you have known I was at work? Besides, it's my* *choice. I'd rather sit and talk to you any day of the week. I work until 10 tonight, which—yuck.*

Cal: *That's a long shift.*

Grey: *Yeah, but it's the only day I work this week. I'm really grateful they're so flexible. Confession? I think the manager has a crush on me or something. It's kind of embarrassing, but it also works in my favor.*

Cal: *I don't blame the guy. Wait. It is a GUY, right?*

Grey: **rolling my eyes*giggle* Yeah, it's a guy. Not nearly as sexy as you ;)*

Cal: *You did NOT just say that.*

Grey: *Oh boy, here we go again…*

chapter seven

Greyson

The espresso machine hisses, and I pour cold, clear water into the top of the machine's water chamber, checking quickly to make sure the boiler cap is secured. My co-worker Rebecca tosses me the filter holder that I'd forgotten to grab when I started to fill the machine with grounds, and I call out a hasty "Thanks" as I lightly brush the coffee debris off the counter that escaped when I changed it earlier.

I remove the glass carafe under the spout and flip the switch on the machine, humming to myself as the steam heats the water to an extra hot temperature—like the customer ordered—and almost don't notice when the coffee starts to overflow into the small carafe. Crap, how on earth did *that* happen?

"Shoot," I murmur as the brown liquid skims the top of the glass container, the foam now becoming white. I push back the lever and remove the cup, careful not to spill any of the precious nectar.

Nectar? Oh, brother, listen to me.

I add a shot of sugar-free vanilla, pour the espresso into the tiny to-go cup, pop the plastic lid on, and slide the beverage across the counter at my waiting customer with a smile.

"Anything else?" I ask.

"Nope!" She tosses her hair over her shoulder and a few pennies into the tip jar, giving me a backwards wave, and pushes her way out the front door.

I reach behind me and pull back on the ribbon securing my green apron, tighten it so it's not quite so loose, and begin wiping down the hard granite counter where we keep the flavor syrups.

As I'm adjusting the nozzle on the sanitizer spray bottle so it comes out in a steady stream, Rebecca scoots by me, giving me a sharp shove in the hip.

"What the hell, Becca?"

"Meathead, twelve o'clock," she mutters, rushing to the cash register. I hear her brightly call out, "Hi there! What can we make for *you* today!"

Wow, she sounds uncharacteristically cheerful.

Shaking my head with a chuckle, I begin spraying the sanitizer around the basin of the steel prep sink, but a deep baritone response from the other side of the cash counter has me stopping in my tracks.

"Grey working?"

I spin on my heel, tossing the rag in my hand to the backsplash. "Cal!" I take a few surprised steps forward. "What are you doing here?"

"I've been doing a shit ton of studying today and needed a break. Grab some caffeine," he says, causally stuffing his hands in the pockets of low-slung sweat pants, then looking up at the menu board on the wall. "Anything good here?"

Delighted, I cannot contain my enthusiasm. "You're an hour away! Are you crazy?"

I'm positively giddy.

Cal looks embarrassed, his cheeks taking on a pinkish hue.

"Didn't we already establish we both have a touch of the crazy?"

A bubble of laughter escapes my lips. "Good point."

Beside me, Rebecca clears her throat loudly. "Uh *hem*."

"Oh! Sorry, Becca. Cal, this is my co-worker Rebecca. She is required to put up with my atrocious barista skills. Becca, this is Cal, my friend. He goes to SMU."

"Cal? *The* Cal? *Boyfriend* Cal?"

Oh, crap, that's right. I give Becca an amused look. "You follow me on Twitter?"

"Uh, everyone follows you on Twitter," she snickers.

This is news to me. "Well, Becca, this is Cal."

"In the flesh," Cal adds gamely, giving her a cocky grin.

"Phew, is it hot in here?" Rebecca blushes down into her black collared shirt. "Okay, well. Since we have no other customers, why don't you go take a break? If it gets swamped—" she rolls her eyes "—I'll shout for you."

Have I mentioned lately how much I freaking *love, love, love* Rebecca?

"Do you want to go sit for a bit?" I ask Cal. He gives a jerky nod. "Can I make something for you quick?"

"Um… how about a trenta green tea lemonade."

"Coming right—"

"—Actually, Grey, I got it," Becca says, cutting me off with a wink. "Go. Sit. The lull isn't going to last forever."

She doesn't have to tell me twice.

Calvin

"I can't believe you're here."

"I can't either," I deadpan. "I got in my truck to grab a coffee and kept driving until I ended up here."

"Just like that, huh?" Greyson is beaming at me, a megawatt smile so blinding it's like gazing at the sun, and I can hardly stand to look at her.

"Um, don't read too much into it," I force myself to say.

"Mmm hmm, okay." She's leaning back now in the stiff wooden chair, her shoe dangling from the foot crossed over her leg. She tilts her head to one side as she studies me, and her long, blonde ponytail—a stark contrast against her black shirt—cascades over her shoulder. "I won't. You just got in your car and drove. For an hour." Grey bats her eyelashes at me.

I blink then look away.

"Stop it," I finally say as Becca walks over, setting a large green tea lemonade on the table in front of me. She doesn't say anything, but I see her mouth *Oh my God* to Greyson before turning and hustling back to the counter.

"I must say, Calvin, if you're trying to dispel the rumors that I have a boyfriend, you're doing a terrible job by showing up here."

"I think you fueled the rumors yourself after that match last week."

"Alright, fair enough. But I wouldn't do anything differently because that kiss was… *phew!*" She props her elbow on the table, resting her chin in the palm of her hand. "My toes are still tingling."

I ignore her blissful sigh and clear my throat.

"I told you, I came here for a coffee."

Her hazel eyes zero in on my green tea lemonade, and she arches a perfect eyebrow.

"Fine, sexy barista, if you really must know, I don't drink coffee."

Greyson's eyes soften around the edges as she watches me fiddle with my straw. "Your bruises are fading," she remarks.

"Yeah, I know. It sucks, too. No one messes with me when I have double shiners."

Grey sits up and reaches across the table, wiggling her fingers in my direction. "Let me have your arm."

I lay a tan arm on the table. She rolls her eyes.

"Not that one. Your other arm."

Biting back a grin, I rest my tatted arm on the tabletop and sit back, watching as she leans forward, intently studying the sleeve on my right arm.

A dozen intricate, bright designs are interwoven on my skin, and she memorizes every single one. I can see the interest in her eyes, the questions. But unlike other girls, she doesn't ask. Her fingers curiously roam over the American eagle tattooed in honor of my grandfather's many years of military service that eventually took his life, the lotus flower tattooed in honor of my mother's winning battle with cancer, and the Celtic cross in honor of my Scottish heritage.

I sit, ramrod straight, learning every expression as it crosses her face.

She glances up at me then, her finger continuing to trail along the sensitive skin on my arm, and there's a fire in her eyes that damn near takes my breath away.

No way is she looking at *me* like that.

Greyson

We sit for twenty minutes before Becca comes to get me, talking and teasing and flirting. Well, I flirted; he complained about it.

"Let me walk you out," I say, stalling for more time with him.

I start untying the green apron strings around my waist, but Cal stops me.

"Leave the apron. It's cute."

I preen with pleasure as he pushes through the glass door of the coffee shop and holds it open for me, giving me an opportunity to train my eyes on that gloriously tattooed bicep beneath his shirtsleeve as I pass in front of him.

His red truck is parked out front, but instead of walking to it, I lead him to a partition under the overhang, conveniently located in the shadows of the strip mall.

I lean against the brick wall, facing him, and cut to the chase. "Tell me the real reason you're here."

He moves into the dark recesses of the building, propping a hand against the partition next to my face, the dim lighting hardening the angles of his face, slashing it in half by shadows. A band of light cuts across his eyes, and they burn bright blue. "I told you. I wanted a study break."

"Okay…"

His face might be cloaked in darkness, but even so, I can tell his eyes are dancing. "Okay what?"

I wish he'd cut the crap. "So, you're here because you were thirsty. And what else?"

He's quiet, watchful, when a dark SUV pulls up with tinted windows. For a few seconds, as it idles, his stance hardens and he moves to stand in front of me protectively. He relaxes when the engine cuts off and a young couple steps down, heading towards the coffee shop.

Finally, in a low murmur, his voice resonates close to my ear in a husky drawl. "You know why I'm here."

"Yes," I agree quietly with a shiver. "But I want to hear you say it."

Cal groans miserably.

"Why won't you just admit you drove all the way here to see me?" I ask gently.

"If you already know the answer, why are you trying to make me say it?"

"Because I'm a girl, and that's what we *do*." My head tips back against the brick wall, and I watch him from under my long lashes. "Hurry up and spit it out. I have coffee to brew."

Minutes on the clock tick by.

"You're a brat."

I push off the building and straighten to my full height as I start towards the door, throwing in a theatrical eye roll to illustrate just how *over* this conversation I am. "I'm going inside. Thanks for stopping by."

I know he's not going to let me go, and two seconds later I'm proven right when my back is pressed flat up against the cold, brick wall.

Greyson 1: Cal 0

Smugly, I let him struggle for the words I crave from him, but this time I don't goad him into talking, even though I know Becca is going to be pissed when I walk back inside after leaving her alone behind the counter for so long.

"You're right." His deep voice whispers next to my ear, and I get chills when he braces those sexy, muscular arms on either side of my face, his breath caressing my cheek. "I drove an hour to see you, and I would have driven three."

God, that is so sexy and romantic.

"Say that again."

He pauses before his palms slide down my shoulders, and his large hands span my waist. "I drove an hour to see you," he repeats, his full lips grazing the soft spot behind my ear. "And I would have driven three."

Oh *yeah*.

My head tilts to the side, my eyes flutter shut, and I almost forget to breath. "Why?"

"Because I can't stop thinking about you."

Cal's lips drag slowly across my jaw, his abrasive beard stubble sending shocks of pleasure up my spine.

God, I love his facial hair. "Say that again."

"I can't stop thinking about you."

My lips curve up into a sly smile. "Good."

World around us forgotten, I exaggerate my pucker, inviting him in. I *ache* with need for him.

We ache with need for each other.

Our lips press together, and for a moment we do nothing but breathe in and out, the same air. The same breath. Cal's full mouth covers mine, deep and…

Tentatively, our tongues touch. Deliberately. So agonizingly unhurried.

I'm breathless now, my knees shaking.

Painful. Arousing. Exciting.

It's wet, and delicious, and incredible.

###

Grey: *I still can't believe you just showed up tonight. I hate to be the one to say it, but… it was really romantic.*

Cal: *You're not mad, are you?*

Grey: *NO! Why on earth would I be?*

Cal: *Just checking.*

Grey: *That kiss was… indescribable.*

Cal: *Yeah, it was pretty incredible.*

Grey: *I don't know how I made it back into work, my legs were all wobbly. I could hardly walk straight.*

Grey: *You showing up was off the charts sexy and romantic—albeit a tad stalker-ish. Totally something I would do if I were one. Which I'm not. But YOU are.*

Cal: *Stop.*

Grey: *IF I did have a stalker, I would want it to be you.*

Cal: *Ditto.*

Grey: *Soooo… Becca thought you were cute… *avoids eye contact and checks nails**

Cal: *What? Cute? Ugh, nooo! Anything but cute! A wise woman once said that CUTE was the "kiss of death" and for grandmas and kittens.*

Grey: *LOL. I did say that, didn't I? But it's true. Because when she said you were cute, I wanted to tackle her to the ground. Haha, kidding.*

Cal: *Are you trying to tell me it made you jealous?*
Grey: *What? Me jealous? Pfft.*
Grey: *Okay, yes. I was jealous.*

chapter seven

Cal: *Morning sunshine.*

Grey: **groans* I can already tell this is going to be a loooong day.*

Cal: *Why is that?*

Grey: *It's only 8:00 in the morning and I've already gotten 3 panic texts from one of my sisters.*

Cal: *Chin up, sweetheart. Text me after your next class, and I'll cheer you up.*

Grey: *You do realize you just called me sweetheart….*

Cal: *I did? Shit, I did.*

Cal: *Sorry?*

Grey: *Did you mean it?*

Cal: *That depends. Did you mind?*

Grey: *No. I liked it. Loved it actually.*

Cal: *Then yes. I meant it.*

Grey: *Awwww *blushes prettily and giggles**

###

Cal: *Has your day gotten any better?*

Grey: *Much better, thanks to you. Starting my day with a text from Calvin seems to always help. But enough about me—how was YOUR day?*

Cal: *It would have been better if my friends weren't such sick sonsabitches. I won't get into details, but let's just say it involved naked ass cracks, lunges, and MY boxer shorts. And the boxer shorts were not on me, but on Mason.*

Grey: *I just laughed out loud, and now my friends all want to know why I'm giggling.*

Cal: *Where are you?*

Grey: *Sitting in the dining hall, having a group lunch on campus.*

Cal: *What did you tell them you were laughing at?*

Grey: *The truth. I told them the truth: that you made me laugh and that you make me happy.*

###

Grey: **yawn* My gosh, why am I so tired?!*
Cal: *You already in bed?*
Grey: *Yes. The pillows were calling my name. You?*
Cal: *Yeah. Reading a book.*

Grey: *Which one?*

Cal: *American Sniper. Have you seen the movie?*

Grey: *Not yet.*

Cal: *We should definitely go see it. I mean—if you want.*

Grey: *Yeah, we should. I'll go anywhere that serves popcorn in a gallon-sized bucket. Do you read a lot?*

Cal: *Yes. I'll read just about anything—except maybe textbooks. Ha ha.*

Grey: *Likes to read: add that to the list of things I like about you.*

Grey: **yawn* Hey Cal?*

Cal: *Yeah, Greyson?*

Cal: *Grey?*

Cal: *Did you fall asleep on me?*

Cal: *Guess so.*

Cal: *Sweet dreams, sweetheart.*

###

Grey: *Morning! I am so sorry I passed out on you last night. Your messages were nice to wake up to, though. Although, somehow I can't picture you calling me sweetheart to my face. Don't tough guys hate that kind of mushy stuff?*

Cal: *Hold that thought, baby cakes. Ha ha. Just got in from my jog. Give me a few to jump in the shower. I'll text you in a bit.*

###

Cal: *Really needed that shower. I did a quick 5 miles. You don't happen to jog, do you? Six Rivers has some sweet trails.*

Grey: *Honestly, no. But I'm willing to try anything once that won't kill me.*

Cal: *Seriously?*

Grey: *Yes. I'll just make sure to run behind you so I can stare at your superb ass #motivation*

Cal: *Hey. You stole my line.*

###

Cal: *Hey Grey?*

Grey: *Yeah?*

Cal: *I'm starting to miss you.*

Grey: *Me too.*

Cal: *You miss you too?*

Grey: *Stop it, you're killing the mood.*

Cal: *Sorry. But I do miss you. Is that weird?*

Grey: *Everything about us is weird.*

Liars

###

Grey: *Tell me something about yourself that no one else knows.*

Cal: *Oh brother, that's horrible. Did you steal that line from a movie?*

Grey: *JUST DO IT*

Cal: *So feisty in the morning—I like it. Okay, fine. But I'm only doing this because although you're small, you're scary. Let's see, something no one else knows. Um. Okay. I have one: everyone thinks I broke my nose playing football, but in reality, it got broken when I was in a fight with my sister.*

Cal: *She was chasing me, and I smashed into a door trying to get away from her. I was 15.*

Grey: *LOLOL >tear< you're so adorable.*

Cal: **rolls eyes* your turn.*

Grey: *Alright, um…I broke up with my last boyfriend, but I let him tell people he broke up with me.*

Cal: *You must have really wanted to get rid of him. When was this?*

Grey: *Freshman year. So, two years ago.*

Cal: *And that's the last guy you dated?*

Grey: *Pretty much. What about you?*

Cal: *I haven't dated any guys in the last two years either.*

Grey: *Would you KNOCK IT OFF?*

Cal: *Why do you keep yelling at me in all caps?*

Grey: *Just answer the question.*

Cal: *Fine. My last "real" girlfriend was a girl I dated in high school. Kid shit, nothing serious. I didn't even take a date to prom; I only went to that because I was on court and my mom made me go.*

Cal: *So, going back to what you said before: if it's been two years since you dated anyone, does that mean…*

Grey: *Does that mean… what? *blank stare**

Cal: *It's a personal question. You don't have to answer.*

Grey: *Go. Spit it out already.*

Cal: *How long has it been? Since.*

Grey: *Ah, now we're getting down to the nitty gritty… How long have you been dying to ask me about sex?*

Cal: *Long enough, smart-ass.*

Grey: *LOL. Okay, so how long has it been since I've had sex—2 long-ass years. Sorry, but I'm not the kind of girl that sleeps around. I'm a committed-relationship kind of person. Does that satisfy your curiosity?*

Cal: *Yes. I like that about you.*

Grey: *Yeah, yeah, yeah. That's what all guys say until they want to have sex with me but refuse to commit. Then they get pissed and never call back. Some guys are so delusional. They think buying a girl one cheap beer is enough to get them into bed. Please, don't make me laugh.*

Grey: *Besides, if you were trying to have sex with me, you wouldn't like it so much either.*

Cal: *I can't like the fact that you don't sleep around? And trust me, I don't need to pressure anyone to sleep with me.*

Grey: *You only like the fact I don't sleep around because it would make you jealous if I did. Let's be honest. ;)*

Cal: *Are you a mind reader?*

Grey: *See, I knew it. Okay. Now you have to answer the same question: How long has it been? Since.*

Cal: *Uh, let me think… Honestly? Maybe 4 months?*

Grey: *Ugh, maybe I shouldn't have asked.*

Cal: *Why?*

Grey: *Because I would have felt much better if you would have said 2 years. LOL. Or lied and said you were a virgin.*

Cal: *Sorry ☹ It was a one-night stand. I can't even remember her name. Wait. Now I do. I think her name was—*

Grey: *STOP! NO DETAILS! My ears will bleed.*

Cal: *Or maybe her name was…*

Grey: *Haha, very funny.*

Cal: *I thought so.*

###

Cal: *Have you crawled into bed for the night yet?*

Grey: *Just. So snuggly. You?*

Cal: *Yeah. Reading and not at all tired. But I miss your face.*

Grey: *You miss my FACE? LOL. Oh my god, you're so cute.*

Cal: *Yup, that's what they call me. Cute.*

Grey: *Want to… Um. FaceTime?*

Cal: *Yeah. Let's do it.*

Grey: *Well, THERE'S a loaded statement. *snickers**

Cal: *I think you might be a bigger pervert than I am.*

Grey: *It's a definate possibility…*

FACETIME

Calvin

I lean back against the headboard of my queen-sized bed and pound my pillows to get more comfortable as my phone pings with an incoming FaceTime notification. Nervously, I wipe my clammy palms across my navy comforter before clicking ACCEPT.

Greyson's beautiful face stares back at me from the small screen. She's lying down, blonde hair fanned out on a white pillow.

"Hi." She gives me a cute little wave, blonde tendrils brushing her cheeks, and she brushes them away, tucking them behind an ear.

"I was beginning to forget what you look like," I tease, eyes devouring her tan, bare shoulders and pink tank top.

"Well, now you won't."

"You know, I don't really do…" I'm momentarily sidetracked by Grey slowly running her index finger along the thin band of her sleep top, adjusting the straps. My eyes are drawn to her lips, then her long, mussed hair. Is she trying to drive me to distraction on purpose?

Her voice interrupts my salivating. "Don't really do what?"

"Huh?"

Her light, lilt-y chuckle fills my room. "What don't you really do?"

"What was I gonna say?" I ask. She shrugs, biting her lower lip. I narrow my eyes. "Knock that cutesy shit off."

"I'm not doing anything!" she shouts with a laugh.

"Stop being irresistible. It's rude."

She rolls her sparkling eyes. "You think *everything* is rude. And why is that?"

"Because I'm here and you're not," I blurt out. "I meant that it's rude you're being cute when I can't touch you. Shit. I didn't mean that if you were here, you'd want me to touch you. Or even want us to be together."

Why am I still talking? Shit.

"Maybe I would, maybe I wouldn't." Greyson lowers her phone so it's hovering just above her face, giving me an extreme close-up. She wiggles her brows. "Are you a cuddler, Calvin," she whispers into the screen.

"Uh, *no*." Her bottom lip juts out in a mock pout. "Yes. Yes I am."

She studies me through the camera on her phone, hazel eyes seemingly raking the planes of my face. "I wish I could touch you. I love your face."

Fuck it. I'm going for broke. "Not as much as I love your face," I announce in a lovey-dovey tone of voice. Seriously, what the hell has gotten into me?

I glance over at my door and make sure it's locked. I so do not need anyone busting in here right now.

"Wanna bet?" Grey teases. She's gazing back at me with doe eyes and an adoring smile, and it's fucking killing me that she's so far away. Well, theoretically speaking, of course. Realistically, it's less than an hour.

"Sweetheart, don't mess with the bull or you'll get the horns," I throw out lamely, trying to be clever but sounding like a complete horse's ass instead. I hold back a whiney groan.

"Horns? That sounds exciting." She wiggles her eyebrows at me.

"Are we flirting?" I ask, to be sure.

"You're hopeless." Greyson laughs. "I don't know about you, but I certainly am." She lolls her head on her pillow and bats her lashes at me through her phone. "You could step it up a notch. You're a little rusty."

"Well, to be honest, I don't usually bother."

"So, what is it you *usually* do?"

"Nothing. I do nothing."

Her pert little nose wrinkles in thought. "Alright, but what if you're trying to... *you know*."

"Get someone to sleep with me?"

She nods, and I let out a deep bark of laughter. Greyson's blonde hair billows out around her head, and she looks like an angel.

"What, like it's hard?" I clear my throat before continuing. "Well. Okay, honestly? Ugh, how do I put this?" I scratch my head. "Girls are easy, okay? All we have to do is show up to a party, and..." I pause for a second. "Yada, yada, yada."

Grey gasps back a surprised laugh, dropping the phone and rolling over on her bed. The phone falls on the bed, camera facing the ceiling—I can't see her, but I can hear her wheezing, "Yada, yada, yada? God, Cal... That was priceless... I love it..."

I wait her out. When she's finally done giggling, she sits up, propping herself up against her headboard, and wipes a tear from the corner of her eye.

"It's good seeing your face," she says quietly. "I haven't seen you in forever."

I feel my expression soften, and I think my goddamn heart just fluttered in my chest. God, I've turned in to a sap.

"It's because we're not, you know—a thing." Why is that so painful to say? Why would I *say* that? Get a grip, dude.

"I know," she says softly. Sadly.

We regard each other silently then, the mood changing from carefree and teasing to serious. Greyson's hazel eyes question me from the small screen on my phone. She tucks her hair behind her ears, almost self-consciously, and we both smile stupidly.

I take a deep breath, gathering up my courage. "Greyson, I—"

Someone bangs on my bedroom door, and just like that, the spell is broken. *Fuck*, fuck, fuck.

"Shit. I should…"

"You should…

"Get that," we both say.

"Talk to you later?" Grey asks into the camera.

Yes. Later.

"Night, Grey."

"Night, Calvin." The quiet, gentle way she says my name, and how she's watching me as I end the call, has me awake all night.

chapter eight

Cal: *Morning, sunshine.*

Grey: *☺*

Cal: *I think my roommates were on to me last night. I think they knew it was you.*

Grey: *How so?*

Cal: *Must have looked guilty after FaceTiming when I opened the door. They heard your voice on speaker phone but were convinced I had a girl in my room. What pains in my ass.*

Grey: *Note to self—if I'm ever in your in your room, hide in closet?*

Cal: *Like I'd ever want to hide YOU.*

Grey: *You are so perfect. Adorable.*

Cal: *Well, you're gorgeous. Does that make us even?*

Grey: *I swear, I want to smush you.*

Cal: *Smush me? God, I hope that's not all?*

Grey: *Well… no.*

Cal: *Shit, we have to stop this. I'm about to walk into a team meeting. I can't be all freaking smiley. I'll get sacked in the nuts.*

Grey: *You are such a prude.*

Cal: *Me, a prude? Hardly. Your plans today?*

Grey: *Meeting with the sisters on my committee to put together donation baskets at the sorority house. It will probably take most of the afternoon. How bout you?*

Cal: *You know, if you weren't busy, I would—*

Grey: *???*

Cal: *I would have come to see you?*

Grey: *I would have loved that if I wasn't so busy today…*

Cal: *Me too.*

Grey: *Sigh.*

###

Cal: *Sleepy?*

Grey: *The sleepiest. I'm glad you texted me though. FINALLY! Why didn't you text me this afternoon? I checked my phone so many times during our meeting that Jemma snatched it away.*

Cal: *I knew you were busy. Didn't want to bother you.*

Grey: *You're the highlight of my day, Calvin. You can text me any time you want *blushes**

Cal: *Ditto, babe.*

Greyson

To: cal.thompson04@smu.il.edu
From: grevkeller0143@state.edu
Subject: *You are cordially invited...*

Dear Calvin,

As you know, the Theta Rho Theta Gala, which I've worked so hard to plan, is right around the corner. Two weeks away, actually. Friday the 9th, 6:00 pm at the Crown Hotel ballroom. I've given this a tremendous amount of thought, and I know it's a lot to ask, but the thing is. The thing *is*, Cal, there is absolutely no one I would rather go with than you. I'm asking you to stand by my side, as my date. Nothing would make me prouder than walking in on your arm. *Yours, Greyson*

I stare at the message, my finger hovering about the SEND button, before I take a deep breath and push down.

Calvin

I'm asking you to stand by my side, as my date. Nothing would make me prouder than walking in on your arm.

Yours, Greyson.

Yours.

Surely she didn't mean it like *that*.

But what if she did?

Shit. I stare at that signature line for what seems like an eternity, reading and rereading her message at least five times before closing out the email app and tapping open my calendar.

And there it is: Friday the 9th. SMU vs. UCONN

It's a huge game for us. Top three match of the entire season, and our season has only just begun. If I miss it, I could very well kiss my Captain's position goodbye, along with my starting position, and say hello to being a second-string bench warmer.

I close the calendar with a curse, and I let my head fall against my bedroom wall with a loud thud.

"Goddammit."

Greyson

"I did something stupid," I say to Melody as she putters around our kitchen, prepping her beloved macaroni and cheese. My arms are braced on the small round table near the stove, and she gives me a quick glance as she measures out milk in a measuring cup.

"I'm listening."

"I invited Cal to the Gala, and he hasn't responded to my message."

"How long ago did you send it?"

"Um, two days ago?"

"So?"

"So, we've been texting and emailing every day for a while."

Melody looks over at me in surprise. "Like *every* day?"

"Pretty much. All day, every day," I clarify with a nod.

"Wow, how did I not know this? Why didn't you say anything?" She asks, ripping open the bag of powdered cheese and tapping it into the pot of noodles.

I shrug. "No reason. Maybe I got carried away with the idea of him. We've been talking for weeks, Mel. *Weeks*. He and I…"

When I look up, she's staring expectantly but says nothing.

"I'm not going to put a label on what I feel for him, but my feelings are real. And they're strong."

That's a lie. I know what to label my feelings for Cal, and those feelings go well beyond strong.

My roommate taps the wooden spoon on the side of the metal pot, sets it on the stovetop away from the burner, and walks over, enveloping me from behind in her arms. "I'm sorry, then, Grey. Sorry that he hasn't gotten back to you. Why don't you send him another note?"

Her chin is resting on my shoulder, and I raise my arm to pat her on the head.

Melody clears her throat. "Alright. Would… would it make you feel better if I sent Mason a note to find out what was going on with him?" she asks bashfully, as if embarrassed to be confessing a secret. "We've kind of been talking. Jemma gave him my digits."

I want to tell her no, but that would be a lie. Another one.

"Could you?"

She squeezes my shoulders. "Sure. You know I'd do anything for you."

###

Melody: *Heard back from Mason. The guys have a match on Friday the 9th and it's a BIG one. I'll forward you his message.*

Melody: [FWD: Mason Gille] *Hey hot stuff. All I can tell you is that Cal's been a real asshole for the past few days. Bitchier than usual. We have a game the same night as your thing and it's a big one. No way would he miss it. Sorry bae.*

Melody: ☹ *I'm so sorry, Grey. Do you want me to ask Brandon Bauer if any of the Tau Kaps would be your date?*

Grey: *No thanks. It's fine. I'll be fine. Love you for thinking of me though* xxx

To: cal.thompson04@smu.il.edu
From: grevkeller0143@state.edu
Subject: Put me out of my misery

Cal,

It's been a few days since my last email, and I'm just writing to tell you that I know you have a match that night. The 9th. I obviously didn't know about it when I asked you to be my date, so I'm sorry if I put any pressure on you by asking. I feel horrible. But why haven't you emailed me back? Why haven't you texted me? It's making me feel really shitty. I thought we were friends, and I thought… Never mind what I thought. Just send me a note back. Because I'm bossy and I say so. And because I miss you so much. Yours, Grey

Cal: *You know what?*
Cal: *Fuck it. I'm coming.*
Cal: *What time should I pick you up?*

###

To: grevkeller0143@state.edu
From: cal.thompson04@smu.il.edu
Subject: Douchebaggery

Grey. I don't think you can begin to comprehend the level to which I'm getting harassed over here for missing this match to come to a dance. Some bastard put tampons in my locker yesterday, and today the ugliest prom dress was hanging from the wakeboard rack on top of my truck, blowing in the wind like a flag. – Cal

To: cal.thompson04@smu.il.edu
From: grevkeller0143@state.edu
Subject: Squeals of delight.

Calvin,

Oh no! That sounds… hilarious, actually. But don't mind me. I'm just delirious with excitement that you're coming. I would love to have seen your face when you opened your locker to tampons. What brand are they? I'd hate to waste a new box. KIDDING. Kidding. Sort of.

I'm not even going to pretend I'm not happy dancing my way around the house. I'm not going to send you "*Oh, Cal! You HAVE to go to your game! Don't miss it on my account!*" notes. Because the truth is, when you texted that you were escorting me to the gala, I squealed so loud Melody burst into my room with a baseball bat. She thought I was being attacked. So, I CANNOT WAIT to see you. I can't wait for you to see my dress. I can't wait to dance with you. And I guess I should mention now that the evening is going to run really, really late. I know SMU is only an hour away, but... Greyson

###

Cal: *Why, Miss Keller, are you propositioning me for an overnight?*

Grey: *Hmmm. Am I? I just meant I know you'll be tired. I have to stay afterwards with my committee and remove some of the sorority insignia and stuff. The hotel staff will do the rest, but there will be a short lag before I can leave.*

Cal: *This is at a fancy hotel, right?*

Grey: *Yup. The Crown Hotel. It's 5 stars.*

Cal: *Wouldn't it just be easier to book a room?*

Grey: *Well, yes, but…*

Cal: *Let me take care of it.*

chapter nine

Greyson

I have a thousand things to do but can only focus on one thing: Cal. Cal, who's skipping his game for me and is surely going to pay the consequences. Cal, who's driving an hour out of his way to be with me. Cal, who calls me sweetheart.

Four times in fact.

I counted.

Sigh.

I scoured online for hours to find this, the perfect dress, and as I stand in front of the mirror, nervously adjusting the invisible neckline with trembling fingers, I stare, trying to imagine how Cal will feel when he first sees me in it.

I didn't just choose the dress with him in mind; I chose it *for* him.

Flesh-colored netting hugs my shoulders so they appear bare, while an intricate white lace overlay creates a cap sleeve and bodice. White embroidered flowers cover the tapered waist, the skirt flaring in a bell at my hips. The dress is both ridiculously sexy and modest at the same time. Rhinestone stud earrings complete the elaborately elegant ensemble.

I run a hand over my hair. The intricately loose fish braid is nestled in a cascade of loose hair and adorned with a vintage white floweret clip. I sat patiently in a salon chair two hours, and the outcome is messy and complex and exquisite.

I love it.

My minimal eye makeup was expertly applied. Dramatic false eyelashes, the darkest mascara, nude shadow. Flushed skin. Bright plum matte lips that are a contrast to my white dress and blonde hair.

I take a deep breath, running a hand over my nervous stomach.

"Whoa! I mean—wow! Seriously, Grey, you look freaking amazing!" Melody floats into the room, her soft pink gown drifting airily around her tall frame. "You look like Blake Lively on the red carpet. Holy wow. Just *stunning*."

"Me? Look at you! Let me see the back," I say, twirling her around to peek at the back of her dress. Or lack of it. "Seriously, Mel, Sam is going to crap himself."

She runs a hand down a front pleat and sighs. "Well, I'm hoping to get a few good pictures taken so I can snap them to Mason. Who is, by the way, totally pissed off at Cal for bailing on their game. Or match. Or whatever they call it."

"What's he been saying?"

Melody smooths a hand over her sleek chignon. "That Cal is pussy whipped."

I try to hide a smile behind my long braid, but the dark plum lipstick gives away my pleased smirk.

"I see that smile, Greyson Keller! Brat." She lets out a wistful sigh. "It's so romantic. He's going to end up on the bench, but Mason says he doesn't even give a shit."

My eyes widen, riveted.

"Yup. Benched. For three games or something like that."

"What else did this endless wealth of knowledge tell you?"

"That he's making a huge sacrifice for someone who hasn't even, uh…"

"Hasn't even… what?"

"You're seriously going to make me say it?"

"I don't even know what *it* is!" I laugh.

"Ugh, fine. He said that Cal is making a huge sacrifice for a guy who hasn't even *fucked you* yet and doesn't even know if the pussy is worth the price tag."

"*What?*" I'm convinced my eyes bug out of my head. "He said that to *you*? What a pig!"

Melody blushes. "Yeah, it was harsh, but all his teammates are seriously pissed. It's blowing up on him; I mean, he's their Captain. Plus Cal didn't tell the guys until after he'd told their coach—who, by the way, was furious. That being said, I'm glad."

Melody walks over and grabs one of my nude colored high heels out of the shoebox, unbuckles it, and squats down so I can slide my foot in. She glances up as she fits the leather ankle strap through the gold clasp. "For the record, it's about time you found a guy with balls big enough to go after what he wants. He basically gave his entire team the proverbial middle finger so he could be with you tonight."

I get warm and tingly all over.

"Anyway, I wish I could be here when he picks you up, but I better skedaddle if I'm going to get the shit done on that list you made me so you could meet Cal here instead of at the hotel. You owe me big time for this, you know. Oh, shoot, I almost forgot. Hand me your overnight bag. I'll take it now so you don't look awkward hauling it out in your fancy dress. Not classy."

"Not classy," I agree, and I wheel the small lavender carry-on suitcase over to the door.

She grabs it, leans to peck me on the cheek, and starts back towards the door. I call her back. "Hey Mel?"

Turning, she regards me. "Yeah?"

"I love you."

"Love you too."

###

Cal: *Just about to leave. I'll see you in an hour. Sooner if I push the gas.*

Grey: *Don't do that! Be safe. Two hands on the wheel. Melody and Jemma are picking up my slack, so there's no rush.*

Cal: *Alright. Be there in an hour.*

Grey: *I can't wait to see you.*

Cal: *Me either.*

Calvin

I pull at my necktie as I take the steps to Grey's front door, tugging it back and forth to tighten the knot I'd loosened on the way over so I could breathe.

It's a white silk tie with white embroidered flowers, a tie my sister picked out when I told her what I was doing, and who I was doing it with. It's also the color of Greyson's dress.

Maybe the guys are right; I am fucking pussy whipped.

But I swear, when Grey finally opens that door, I don't give one shit what anyone says. They can bench me or filet me alive or kick me off the team, for all the fucks I care.

Because Greyson is stunning.

And the look she's giving me right now has me standing twenty feet tall.

Greyson

For a moment, we just stare at one another.

It's me who moves first, opening the door wide enough for Cal to step through, up into the living room.

He looks so handsome. Black pleated dress pants, crisp black shirt, tailored black jacket, and a glaringly white embroidered tie that matches my dress perfectly.

I want to touch him.

"Jesus, babe, let me look at you," he says with a strained voice, stepping farther into the room. "You are so *beautiful*."

"I *feel* beautiful." I give a pleased little twirl, and my skirt flares up around my hips. His eyes go to my bare legs, and I bite back a smile as I say, "I need a hug or something."

Or *something*.

Cal smiles, shrugs off his suit coat, lays it neatly over a kitchen chair, and wraps his arms around my waist after I step into his outstretched arms. I lean into the embrace, mindful not to get makeup on his shirt.

My lips graze his jaw, tattooing his skin with plum lip prints, and I draw back, fingering his tie. It matches my dress.

I gasp with delight. "Wherever did you find this?"

"Tabitha." He rolls his eyes. "She literally lost her shit when I asked for her help. It made her whole year. But then my mom got all weird because I didn't call her first. It was a whole *thing* I'd rather not talk about," he jokes. "Tabitha had it rush shipped to school. She can't believe I'm going to a sorority formal and wants to meet the girl putting up with my bullshit for an entire night— her words, not mine."

"Well, thank your sister for me because you look… Is it possible that you got more handsome since the last time I saw you? How am I going to keep my hands to myself?"

"You don't have to keep your hands to yourself," he jokes.

"Okay. I won't."

"In that case, I guess I'll have to send my sister a bouquet to thank her for making me irresistible."

"Maybe you should."

We stare at each other until I'm itching to run my fingers down his chest. Instead, I flex them and state the obvious. "We should go. Melody is covering for me, and I can't leave her hanging or she'll *kill* me. I promised I'd be there by five thirty."

Calvin

When she's not leaning in to hug or shake someone's hand, Greyson's arm is looped through mine, her hand clasping my tricep as we stand at the head of a receiving line, enthusiastically greeting the Gala's arriving guests: sorority alumnae, her sorority sisters, and their dates.

I cannot stop giving her sidelong glances, for she is truly a vision.

It's over an hour before we're "alone" and Greyson can take a break from her hostess duties. I set my beer glass on a nearby table, and we wordlessly move out onto the hardwood dance floor. I pull her in close, and her fingers snake under my suit jacket, clasping at the small of my back.

I want to kiss her so badly right now, but it's not the time or place. I settle for resting my lips on her neck, just below the white flower she has pinned there, running my hands up and down her spine.

We dance like this through one song, then another. I've never been more grateful to hear a bunch of cheesy slow songs in my life.

Because somehow… we just *fit*.

And fuck if it doesn't feel amazing.

Greyson

At this point, I don't even think we're moving. Cal's nose is buried in my hair, his fingers are stroking my back, and when the chords from the next slow ballad begin, I don't even care that I have responsibilities to see to.

Just one more song, and I'll go pull the silent auction bid cards.

One more.

Or two. I can afford two more songs.

My hands find their way up the front of his shirt, resisting the urge to pop open the row of black onyx buttons one at a time. Those same hands wrap around his neck, resting there so my delicate fingers can rake through the curly hair just above his starched black collar.

Cal kisses my temple and tightens his hold, his hot breath on my neck throughout the song.

I continue stroking his hair. He rubs my back in a light caress.

I'm sure we look ridiculous just standing here, barely dancing, but I still feel like I'm floating on air.

"I don't know if I mentioned it, but thank you for coming tonight," I aimlessly twirl a piece of his hair around my finger.

His voice is a hum next to my ear. "You've only mentioned it four or five times. But for the record, there's no other place I'd rather be."

I whisper against his skin. "I won't ever take you for granted, Cal. I know the sacrifice you made to be here tonight."

"I know."

I arch back and cock my head at him. "Is your sister horrified you're at a sorority formal?"

His mouth curls up into a smirk. "I wouldn't say horrified; I'd call it shocked. I mean, I'm not really the type to, you know…"

I nod. "I know." We sway to the music, and his hands rest on my hips. "Speaking of types, what is yours?"

"Oh, gee, let me think," he laughs. "Blonde hair, hazel eyes, infectious smile…"

I nuzzle our noses.

Sick, I know.

"You think I have an infectious smile?" I smile at him.

"And kissable lips."

"Ooh! Now *that* I like the sound of." I release my fingers from his silky mop of hair, trail them over his shoulders and down over his firm pecs, and give them a squeeze. He puckers his lips, and I touch my trout pout to his—briefly, so I don't smear my lipstick.

Cal rolls his head to the side and groans. Loudly. "I want to, *ugh*. So bad."

Laughing, I press my lips to his for another quick kiss. "Want to what?"

"Never mind. I'll sound like a dog in heat if I say it."

My heartbeat quickens. "Say it anyway," I plead.

He hesitates. "I want to stick my fucking tongue down your throat."

"I want that too," I murmur, leaning in to flick his ear with my tongue. "I want to lick you from head to toe."

"Fuck. Um, okay. You win." He gives a strangled laugh and buries his face in my neck. "I cannot believe you just said that."

"Why?"

"Because. You look so sweet. And you're classy."

"Hmm," I hum in his ear as we sway, enjoying the power of my femininity when his whole body stiffens at the simplest inflection of my tone. "Well, you know what they say about the classy ones."

"No." His voice squeaks slightly. "What do they say?"

I raise one eyebrow suggestively.

His head shoots up, eyebrows in his hairline. "My dick is so hard right now." He groans. "Shit. Sorry, I shouldn't have said that out loud."

"Hard? Ya *think*? It's been digging into my thigh this entire time. Trust me, it's taking every last effort for me not to grind on it."

"Jesus, Grey!" Our bodies are flush, and Cal is pushing his hips into me slightly. Not enough to be obvious to an onlooker, but enough that I notice. "I'm trying really, really hard to be polite."

"Polite boys deserve a reward." My warm breath flirts with his square jawline, his dark blonde hair tickling my nose. "You know what that means, don't you?"

He gives his head a jerky shake. "No. What does that mean?" The Adam's apple in his throat bobs up and down when he swallows.

"Thompson, it means you're getting *lucky* tonight."

###

"Um… You were seriously steaming up the dance floor. For a fake boyfriend, it sure did look real." Melody sidles up to me by the cake table, whispering around a stack of dessert plates and nodding politely at each passing guest. "Jeez, sexual tension much?"

"Tell me about it. And I don't think there's anything fake about it anymore," I whisper back, smiling broadly at a new member of our sisterhood when she comes up for a slice of the marble cake Mel and I are cutting.

We make small talk with her and serve several more pieces of cake before we're able to speak alone again. "Grey, you two look like you're…" She hesitates, and the cake knife she's wielding pauses mid-slice. "You know—in *lurve*."

I consider this, glance across the room where Cal stands with a group of some older gentleman—alumnae dates and husbands—gesturing wildly and causing everyone to die laughing uproarishly.

I wonder what's so funny.

He raises a drink to his lips just then and glances over, watching me above the rim of his glass. I blush furiously before looking away.

A knot forms in the pit of my stomach. Oh God, I'm actually jealous that I'm stuck on the opposite side of the room serving stupid, dumb cake.

"Geez Grey, look at you, all flustered and a*dork*able."

"I can't help it. He makes me positively giddy. I'm head over heels."

"Yeah, I can tell. And I think the feeling is mutual. That boy hasn't stopped watching you all night. But I mean—who could blame him. You're clearly the babeliest babe in the room." The cake knife is thrust my way. "And I'm not just saying that because you're my best friend."

"Yes you are, but I'll permit it."

"What are your plans for later? You check in to your room yet?"

"Yeah, Cal took care of it while I was helping Carly and Jemma with raffle tickets."

"Nervous?"

"No. We've been building to this point for over seven weeks. *Seven*. I want to kick everyone out and drag him upstairs, caveman style. Like, by his beautiful hairs." I sigh wistfully and hand her a stack of napkins. "Lick."

Melody covers her laugh with a cake plate. "Oh gawd, if only he knew how dirty your mind was, he wouldn't be so content chatting it up over there with Stella's husband Ryan."

"Well, he kind of *does* know. I may have whispered some naughty, dirty things to him while we were dancing."

"Such as…?"

"Such as, 'I want to lick you from head to toe.' I think he almost wet himself."

"Why are you let loose to roam around in public?"

"It's not like I say things like that to just anyone. Besides, I just wanted to see the look on his face. It's totally different."

"Yeah, yeah, whatever you say, Keller. Now keep handing me plates."

chapter ten

Calvin

By midnight, we begin making our way back to our room. It's late, but my body crackles with electricity, buzzing with seven weeks' worth of anticipation. A burst of pure adrenaline zips through my body, fueled by Greyson's words as they play on a loop through my mind.

It means you're getting lucky tonight, it means you're getting lucky tonight, it means you're getting lucky tonight…

Arms wrapped around each other's waists, we walk side-by-side in companionable silence and pent-up sexual tension to our hotel suite, taking the elevator to the eighth floor from the Grand Ballroom.

Grey relaxes against me as we watch the numbers climb from one floor to the next.

The elevator dings, having reached its destination, and we step out, make a right turn, and quickly arrive at our door. Grey rests her back against the wall, watching as I dig the room key out of my suit coat and slide the keycard through the card reader.

She leans forward as I turn the doorknob, and I pause, pressing against her gently for a quick kiss. The door eases open, and she sweeps inside, reaching up to pull the flower clip out of her hair and laying it on the dresser. Next to the dresser is the suitcase I placed there earlier.

"I should probably get out of this dress before taking my make-up off," she says from the other side of the room, clicking on a lamp.

My nerve endings strum high on vibrate.

It means you're getting lucky tonight, it means you're getting lucky tonight, it means you're getting lucky tonight…

"Help with my buttons?" Grey turns towards me, presenting her back, holding her lustrous blonde hair aside, and glancing at me over her shoulder.

It means you're getting lucky tonight, it means you're getting lucky tonight, it means you're getting lucky tonight…

In two long strides, I'm reaching for the pearl buttons at the top of her dress, the gentle illusion collar at the nape of her neck a stark distinction to my large, battered calloused hands, and I briefly pause to regard the juxtaposition of them against her dress.

One by one, I pluck the buttons free, and when I'm done, I splay my hands over her smooth back, running them up her spine before brushing her hair aside and pressing my mouth against her skin. Pushing the sleeves of the sheer fabric down her arms, my lips kiss a trail down the tantalizing column of her neck.

Grey shivers, lolling her head to the side with a loud, labored moan as her dress lands in a pile of crinoline and lace at her feet. I take her hand, and she steps out of it, leaving it in a lacy puddle.

Her hazy eyes watch me intensely as I kneel and bend her knee. Unbuckling the straps of her sexy nude heels, I slip them off one at a time, then run my hands up her smooth leg, planting a kiss on the inside of her arched thigh.

I trace a path of kisses up her leg, running my hands up her lean torso. She's standing in only a white pair of lacy underwear and a strapless white bra; one that pushes her sexy tits together until they threaten to spill over the edge of the cups.

It pains me, but I stand, releasing her so she can use the bathroom.

She cups my chin in her palm. "Be right back. Don't go anywhere."

"Not in a million fucking years."

This earns me another kiss, and a second later I get to watch her retreating, toned ass sashaying towards the bathroom.

Sexy as hell.

Biting back a groan, I set to removing my own shoes, followed by my socks, tie, and belt, draping them over the single chair in the room. I untuck my black dress shirt, plucking the buttons opens and letting it hang open.

I heft Greyson's small suitcase up onto the dresser so she won't have to struggle with it later, before removing the cell phone from my pocket and checking it for messages.

There are four text notifications.

Mason: *Thunder cunt. I sure-as-shit hope this chick is worth the shit storm coming your way. We got our asses handed to us tonight, no thanks to you.*

Aaron: *Hey condom breath, you're fucking your stalker right now, aren't you, asshole? I want all the nasty dirty details.*

Aaron: *Sorry. That was really out of line. Don't listen to me. I'm totally shit-faced and probably a little jealous.*

Tabitha: *Hey little brother. How's it going so far? Did Greyson like the tie? GOOD LUCK TONIGHT! She is one lucky girl!*

The text from my sister is the only one that makes me smile—the others make me scowl—so I shoot Tabitha a reply.

Me: *Night went great. You were right about the tie. She loved it. Says to thank you.*

Liars

Then, knowing there's only one way to get her to leave me alone, I add more.

Me: *Stop texting. Speaking of lucky, I'm about to get laid—her words, not mine.*

My sister immediately replies.

Tabitha: *You're disgusting.*

Me: *Whatever.*

I smirk, hitting SEND before powering my phone down and tossing it on the dresser next to my wallet and car keys.

I'm standing in the middle of the hotel room when the bathroom door opens, and Grey emerges wrapped in a fluffy white hotel robe, fresh-faced and glowing, her face free of makeup. Her lips are still stained from her deeply pigmented lipstick. She's removed the pins from her hair; it cascades down her back in loose waves created by the braid.

She's so un-fucking-believably gorgeous.

I try to say something, but no words come out. I'm crazy for this girl.

Grey's hazel eyes widen as she purposefully strides towards me on a mission, eyes on the exposed skin under my unbuttoned shirt. My body goes ramrod straight, and I inhale sharply with breathless anticipation as her smooth palms connect with the planes of my bare chest, fanning out over my pec muscles under my open dress shirt. Unable to prevent myself from flexing, my pecs contract beneath her roaming fingers, and I watch her face, transfixed as her pupil's dilate.

"Your turn. Go clean up and… come to bed," she whispers huskily as her fingertips skim, feather light, over my shoulders and push the black shirt down my arms, over my biceps, until it joins her dress.

Greyson parts her lips.

Her tongue darts out to moisten them.

The shirt drifts silently to the floor. My nipples harden under her soothing touch, and I fight the urge to moan.

Come to bed. Come to bed. Come to bed. Jesus. Do three sexier words even exist in the English language? If so, I sure as shit haven't heard them.

I nod incoherently, my head dipping up and down like a bobble head, putty in her hands. Right now I would literally do *anything* this girl asked me to.

Anything.

Once inside the bathroom, I make quick work of taking a piss, washing my face, and brushing my teeth. Several sexy, dark burgundy lip prints line my jaw.

I leave them.

Taking a deep breath, I open the bathroom door with a shaking hand.

Greyson

I'm not nervous.

Nope, not one bit.

I hear the sink running in the bathroom, and I glance at myself in the mirror above the dresser before unzipping the purple suitcase Cal has thoughtfully removed from the floor for me.

Loosening the belt of the hotel robe, I slide it low on my shoulders and take a few deep cleansing breaths to compose myself and calm my racing heart as I continue to study my reflection; color high, my eyes are bright and slightly wild. Aroused.

I finger a pink sleep shirt in my suitcase, rubbing it while I debate: on one hand, if I don't put a shirt on, I might look cheap and easy. On the other, I did already tell him he was getting lucky, so why bother putting on clothes?

Ugh, crap. I'm *crap* at this.

It's been two years since I've had sex. Two. Years. And quite honestly, I don't ever recall those experiences being particularly memorable.

The robe peels open farther, and the lacy white g-string undies and pristine white bra peek through.

Maybe I'll just…

…let it fall open. Like this?

No, like *this*.

Just then, Cal emerges from the bathroom, and I watch, spellbound, as his hard body advances to the center of the room, clad only in a pair of loose-hung gray sweatpants. You know the ones; they dip low on a guy's hipbones and hug him in all the *right* places.

I can't see it, but I know they're emphasizing his fine, round, athletic ass….

Every firm muscle on his body, every jaded scar, every line of his colorful tattoos are there for my perusal, and boy do I look my fill. He moves closer, watching me through hooded, lust-filled eyes before turning and depositing his folded suit pants on the dresser.

His eyes grow wide at the sight of me standing next to the dresser, first with total shock, then with desire. Hunger.

Want.

Need.

But that's not all I see there.

This guy wants to let himself love me; I can see it in the way he's looking down at me. Like I'm a precious, cherished thing.

I'm not nervous.

Nope, not one bit.

Calvin

I don't know what I did to deserve this girl, but…

Fuck.

Rugby.

Rooted in spot next to the dresser, Greyson faces me, the white robe a contrast to her tan skin, its gaping sliver baring her white bra and panties. She reaches to loosen the knot on her belt farther, the terrycloth falling completely open.

I stare.

I stare at her beautiful body, her waterfall of blonde hair, her high, round breasts and curvy hips. She's not perfect, but she's perfect to me.

"Cal," she entreats quietly, her voice filled with desire. Hunger.

Want.

Need.

For me. For fucking *me*.

I don't know who moved first, but our mouths meet, and my hands span her waist, kneading her bare, warm skin. Provocative. Achingly slow, our hot tongues mingle, wet and wanting.

Wet kisses. Open-mouthed kisses. Lips, tongue and teeth.

Grey's robe falls to the floor, and she breaks the kiss to skim my abs with the tips of her fingers and the waistband of my pants, untying the white knot holding them around my hips.

My dick throbs so hard I can feel it beating in my pants.

Fuck.

I walk her backwards to the bed, the back of her knees hitting the mattress. She lies down, the gold comforter providing a backdrop for her magnificent blonde hair that pools around her fresh, flushed face.

The look she gives me invites me to look. To taste.

To touch.

I crawl on top of her then, dragging an open palm and my tongue up her stomach, over her breasts.

She pants when I lick her cleavage, my wet tongue flicking the groove between her blessedly plump tits. My fingers briefly toy with the small white clasp in front of her bra, and without preamble, I pop it open.

My mouth covers her then, and she moans loudly, her hips wiggling impatiently beneath me. I grind my erection into the apex of her spread thighs. Grind into her hard.

It's torture.

She grabs a handful of my disheveled hair and tugs.

"Lights on or off," I ask between sucking on her flawless skin.

"On. I want to watch you."

"I'm going to make you feel so fucking good, Grey."

"You already have, baby." She gasps into my mouth. "So fucking good."

Baby. Jesus Christ, it sounds good spilling from her lips. The dirty talk. I bite my cheek to stop the litany of endearments threatening to spill off the tip of my tongue, wanting to call her every goddamn mushy name I can think of: baby, sweetheart, sweetie, honey, babe, cutie pie, darling.

Shit. My friends were right; I am pussy whipped.

But only a spineless dickhead would give a shit what his friends thought.

"God, you're fucking sexy as shit," I whisper, caressing her hip. "I love your skin. I love your tits." To illustrate my point, I lick them both, sucking on the dusky nipples.

"Keep talking. What else," she asks, panting in a long, drawn out breath. "You feel so good." It sounds like she's sulking.

"I love how funny you are." Grey tips her head back as I suck on her neck gently, palming her breasts with my now trembling hand, kissing my way down her collarbone. "I love how smart and clever you are."

"You feel so good, Cal. Did I say that already? I'm losing my mind."

"You make me crazy." I moan, totally losing control of the situation. "Do I make you crazy?"

Our incoherent, sex-induced babble fills the room.

"Oh yeah, so crazy." Her hands push frantically at the waistband of my pants, and together, we slide them down my hips, then set to tearing off her underwear in a heated frenzy.

"God, just give it to me, Cal. I don't want to wait anymore; I want you so bad," she implores, reaching for my hard erection, stroking it up and down with her talented fingers. "Don't you want this inside me? I do. I want it bad."

Holy hell. Holy shit, the dirty mouth on her.

"Stop. Don't, baby," I beg through clenched teeth. "Or I'm gonna come."

"Come inside me," she moans, grabbing my ass and pulling me down. My dick brushes the slit of her pussy, pre-cum making it slick. "Please. I'm on the pill. Honey, please. I want this with you so bad."

Pill. *Honey*. Please.

I try to make sense of the words in my brain, but I've lost the function of reasoning.

Shit. *Shit, shit, shit.* I've never had sex without a condom—then again, I've never been serious about anyone before. Ever. Not even close.

But I am now—and whatever she wants I'm going to give her: Commitment. A relationship. Date nights. My cock inside her without a condom.

I swallow the lump in my throat and my balls tighten, eager and twitching with greedy anticipation.

"If we fuck without a condom, Greyson, you're mine. Do you understand?" My plea is hoarse, raw and full of emotions I didn't know I was feeling. "The only person I'd ever consider screwing without protection would be a steady girlfriend."

Or future wife, but I keep *that* shit to myself.

"Silly boy." Greyson cups my cheek in her palm tenderly, even as her rotating hips work the tip of my dick. "I decided I was keeping you the day you showed up at my door. You're *mine*."

Greyson

He feels so good.

So unbelievably good.

Words spill out of his lips. My lips. Incoherent rambling. Babbling. Endearments.

Begging.

Cal slides in and out of me and, "Oh God." I moan, spreading my legs wider as his hips pump, giving it to me good. So, so good. "Deeper, Cal, *push*. Yeah, yes, right there."

My head rolls to the side and I lie like a rag doll as he drives into me, the sensation of his bare flesh against mine almost unbearable. *Ooohhh yeahhh. Uuhhh.* Cal.

"Shit, oh shit. God, this feels amazing. Fucking incredible, baby. I… I… You're my best friend, baby," he confesses in an emotional, choked whisper. "I think I love you." He blurts out this sentiment as a choke gets stuck in his throat.

"I know, I know," I chant. My mouth finds his earlobe and I suck. "I love you too."

Love. What a word. We can't stop saying it.

Can't stop.

"I am. I'm fucking in *love* with you, Greyson." He swivels his pelvis and grinds me down into the mattress.

"I love you, Cal. So much." The words spill out of my mouth in a sob before I can analyze the consequences of our slurred confessions.

Cal's giant hands reach under me, and he grasps my ass, pushing deep.

Our mouths meet then, and we burn for each other. *Burn.* With each kiss and every touch, we worship as only two people who've just declared their love for each other can—with passion and restraint and tenderness.

And once you've said those three little words, a floodgate opens, and you never want to stop saying them. So we don't. We say them again and again, in whispers and whimpers and groans and throaty sighs.

It's raw and deep and *real*.

It would be nauseating if it weren't us.

"I love you," Cal groans again as his hips pump and he slides slowly in and out of me. "Fuck, you feel good, Greyson. So *fuuuu*... sexy. Shit. *Uh*, Grey, I love you, baby."

He's way too gentle. He's way too slow.

My fingers move down his sweaty spine and squeeze his firm ass. "Harder, Cal. I said *harder*. Yes, right there, baby. Don't stop. I love you, I love you. Oh God, *deeper*. Harder. Cal."

Our lips and bodies tell a story, one we've been writing for the past seven weeks… a story of our friendship, bond, and love.

Calvin

Holy shit.

My girl loves me.

My girl loves it deep and hard and dirty and loud.

And that's how I give it to her.

Greyson

We don't stop until we're both panting and sweaty and exhausted.

And then we do it again.

chapter eleven

@Grey_VKeller Tweeted: *I'm officially someone's #girlfriend and off the market #facebookofficial*

@tightheadthompson Tweeted:

@grey_vkeller *damn straight*

@Grey_VKeller Tweeted:

@tightheadthompson *I love you*

@tightheadthompson Tweeted:

@grey_vkeller *I love you too, baby*

@JemmaGemini Tweeted:

@tightheadthompson @grey_vkeller *Gross. Stop. NO ONE wants to see this crap. NO ONE* #tmi #gag #wordvom

@MasonGille32 Tweeted:

@tightheadthompson *Hey* #jerkoff *did we NOT just talk about keeping this* #shit *to yourself? TMI dude* #hornybastard

@Grey_VKeller Tweeted: @JemmaGemini *WHAT THE HECK JEMMA - we're literally sitting across from each other at the same table* #LOL

@JemmaGemini Tweeted: @grey_vkeller *Exactly! GET BACK TO WORK* stop #daydreaming

###

Cal: *You miss me already, don't you?*

Grey: *Yes. Remind me again why you had to leave so early this morning?*

Cal: *Post-game team meeting from last night's match. Of course I got my ass chewed out by at least four people. It wasn't pretty. Coach called me a 'cocksucking little prick' at least twice.*

Grey: *That's so horrible! What did you do???*

Cal: *He flew off the handle when I told him I didn't play because I was getting my priorities straight.*

Grey: *Aww, Cal!*

Cal: *It also didn't help that they got their asses handed to them, which of course is my fault because I wasn't there.*

Grey: ☹ *My poor baby. Is now the time I say I'm sorry?*

Cal: *You're worth the ball busting. Trust me.*

Grey: *You say the sweetest things!!! What are you doing now?*

Cal: *Waiting for the guys. Short practice, the gym, then they want to grab pizza and beer or some shit. You?*

Grey: *Boxing up all the table decorations. Taking everything back to the sorority house for storage. Probably grab dinner and a movie with a few of my sisters. Saturday night, so they'll want to go out.*

Cal: *Stay away from the ass grabbers.*

Grey: *There's only one guy I want touching my backside, but he's got plans tonight. I'll do my best to stay away from the rest of them*

Cal: *You should probably wear a plastic garbage bag over your outfit. And a big hat. Ugly yourself up a bit.*

Grey: *LOL. Now who sounds jealous?*

Cal: *Me, dammit. I am.*

Grey: *Baby, haven't you figured it out yet? I love you. You have nothing to be jealous of...*

###

Grey: *You downtown yet?*

Cal: *Not yet. Sitting here on the couch playing Xbox. Aaron and Tom are both in the bathroom bathing in the same cheap cologne.*

Grey: *Speaking of cologne, have I mentioned lately how good you smell?*

Cal: *No. Tell me again.*

Grey: *Amazing. You smell amazing. Like a clean, woodsy, sexy boyfriend. Mmm. Seriously yummy boyfriend.*

Cal: *I can't fucking believe I have a girlfriend.*

Grey: *It has its benefits.*

###

Grey: *This bar is packed. Not even fun.*

Cal: *What are you wearing?*

Grey: *A plastic garbage bag and a large floppy hat. I look really ugly. You?*

Cal: *Sunglasses, a baseball hat, and an old winter coat.*

Grey: *Perfect.*

Cal: *Remind me again why I'm out with these dipshits and not with you? Why are you there and not here? With me?*

Grey: *Because you're a dumb boy.*

Cal: *Sounds about right.*

###

Grey: *Let's play a game?*

Cal: *Fine. Beats watching these putzes make asses of themselves. I'm pulling up a barstool. Pick your poison.*

Grey: *20 Questions. You start.*

Cal: *Hmmm. Um. Okay. Favorite Color*

Grey: *That's your question? My favorite color is yellow. Yours? Also, next question: boxers or briefs?*

Cal: *My favorite color is—duh—grey. I prefer boxer briefs. Next question: Favorite spot to be kissed.*

Grey: *Thong. Favorite spot to be kissed: on the neck. Next question: Last thing you licked.*

Cal: *What the fuck, Grey!*

Grey: *LOL. Answer the question.*

Cal: *Oh my God, woman, you're killing me. Fine. My favorite spot to be kissed besides my *pointing down there* would be my chest. Last thing I licked? Beer foam.*

Cal: *Question 5. Um. Favorite spot for a first date?*

Grey: *Was that a hint? Cause if it was…*

Grey: *Wait. I have to play catch-up here. Last thing I licked: cupcake earlier today at the sorority house. Delicious. But not as delicious as you. Favorite spot for a first date? Out on the lake. Question: Last thing you WISH you'd licked.*

Cal: *Okay, that's not fighting fair. You wanna play dirty, little girl? Fine. Last thing I wish I licked? You. All over. Tits, ass, everywhere.*

Grey: *Are you trying to shock me? Because it won't work. You'll have to do better than that.*

Grey: *Crap. Some guy just spilled beer all over my shoes. Running to wipe them off. BRB.*

Cal: *Seriously? NOW? Dammit.*

Cal: ...

Cal: *??? UGH!!*

Grey: *Okay, I'm back. Sorry, I know that was a total buzzkill. Last think I wish I'd licked? Your tattoo looks like I want my tongue on it. Next question is yours, slacker.*

Cal: *Alright. Favorite body part on the opposite sex (and I'm going to ignore the tongue on my tattoo comment because if I don't, I'll get hard.)*

Grey: *Question amended. Favorite body part on YOU. Your tight ass, specifically in those gray pants you wore to bed last night. I mean. Orgasmic. Seriously. Your abs are insane.*

Cal: *STOP. Just stop. You're making me hard.*

Grey: *Yeah, well. I guess SOMEONE should have invited me to join him tonight and we could have taken care of that problem. Let's call your hard-on a punishment for being too wussy to ask me out.*

Cal: *That's hitting below the belt.*

Grey: *Below the belt. Mmm mmm… yum.*

Cal: *Knock that shit off. I'm in public. One of my teammates has been trying to steal my phone for the last ten minutes. Says I'm looking down at it like a horny bastard.*

Grey: *Are you?*

Cal: *Yes.*

###

Cal: *We never did finish that game of 20 Questions. Are you still up?*

Grey: *Yeah, we got home about 30 minutes ago.*

Cal: *Sober?*

Grey: *Yes. You?*

Cal: *Yup. FaceTime?*

chapter twelve

3 Weeks Later

Tabitha Thompson

I cannot believe my brother brought a girl home to my parents' house.

I cannot freaking believe my brother has a *girlfriend*.

I wasn't sure I should believe Cal when he first started subtly telling the family bits and pieces about her. Greyson is smart and funny and caring and sweet, blah, blah, blah.

Gag.

Nice and sweet and caring and funny? Pfft! No way. Don't guys *always* say shit like that when they're finally getting laid on a regular basis?

And, of course, being a good sister, I didn't believe he was actually dating anyone. *Especially* when he showed me her picture.

Jeez.

At first, all I could do was stare back at her photographs online and gawk. *That beautiful blonde girl is my brother's girlfriend?* No. Way. Long, naturally blonde hair, big boobs, athletically toned, Greyson Keller is a walking, talking anti-stereotype on two perfectly tanned legs. She actually exists.

In nature. Like, they let her just walk around in the wild.

Greyson Keller is also, I'm happy to report, amazing. Wonderful. Sincere. Real. The whole gamut of pleasant compliments. And more importantly, completely head over heels for my dumb little brother, who deserves someone like her in his life.

I trail behind them, the three of us paddling across the surface of Lake Walton, slicing our oars through the dark water at a leisurely pace, the day calm, sunny, and perfect. Greyson and Cal are ahead of me, rowing side by side in companionable silence.

I watch as they steal glances at each other every couple feet, trying to be sly about it but failing miserably. They cannot keep their eyes off each other, and if I weren't so damn happy for my brother, I would be repulsed.

Nonetheless, as a single female, I feel it's my duty to give an eye roll towards the blue, cloudless sky.

"Babe, let's check out that sand bar over there." My brother's low voice carries back to me. He twists his lean torso and looks back at me. "Tab, we're gonna stop at the island."

"Hey, I know that place!" Greyson exclaims, excited. "This is the little paradise you texted me a picture of."

Cal grins at her, obviously pleased that she remembered, and we all paddle deftly towards the little island. It's actually more of a peninsula jutting out into the water, with a white sand beach, picnic tables, and campfire site.

As we get closer, I can see a small smokestack where the last campers had their bonfire, the faint, gray smoldering cloud rising into the canopy of trees from the dying embers.

My brother continues. "I've always wanted to stop, but stopping by myself always just seemed depressing.

Greyson smiles at him prettily. "Well, now you never have to."

I watch as my brother's steely gaze lands on the cleavage beneath her life jacket. "Kayaking with you is almost worse."

Her pretty eyes widen. "What! Why?"

"Because I just keep wanting to lean over and pull you into the water. Get us both wet."

Gross. I want to splash them both with my paddle. "Alright, you two, stop. Just stop. You're making me sick."

My brother, who I would never guess in a million years would freely give PDA, leans his muscular, tattooed arm out to draw Greyson's kayak closer, and he bends over the side of his, puckering his lips.

Their eyes close behind their sunglasses and their lips meet, pressing together over the water.

They both sigh.

Greyson lays her paddle across her red kayak, the delicate fingers of one hand reaching up to gently stroke the new gash under my brother's left eye. "I have to put some more Neosporin on this." Her voice drifts over the water, soothing.

My annoying brother nods into her palm, gazing at her like a lovesick puppy dog. "Okay."

What the…

Seriously, could this get any worse?

"I brought us a picnic."

Never mind. It just did.

Greyson gasps in delight. "Oh my God, Cal, sweetie—could you be any more perfect?"

"I don't know. Could you?"

"I love you."

"I love *you*."

They're disgusting. Just disgusting.

Greyson sighs.

I sigh too.

It's gonna be a long. Ass. Day.

ACKNOWLEDGEMENTS

Have you ever met anyone online and fallen in like?

Fallen into a relationship with someone you've never even met face-to-face?

I have.

And it's amazing. Hilarious.

I'm talking about my friends; each and every crazy one of them. The ladies in the BS Group online, whom I've never met but am unconditionally faithful to— once they call you asshole, you're golden for life.

Not a day goes by that you don't brighten my day, make me blush, gasp in outrage when you tag me in an inappropriate meme #ShirlRickman, or call me the "W" word; which somehow always feels like a compliment.

Thank you, all you beautiful strangers, for your support. You make my day.

Every day.

M.E. Carter—you're easily becoming like a sister I love to poke in the back seat of the car; constantly pretending to be irritated, but secretly loving every minute of it. In fact, I bet you're grumbling as you read this even though I'm showering you with praise. I've said it before, and I'll say it again: Thank you for friending me, answering all my questions, and for all the introductions. You are a blessing—*a lovely, wonderful, and witty blessing*—and I look forward to many more projects with you.

To Murphy Rae. *Meow.*

You endure endless questions and are always gracious. Yes, you. Gracious. Well. Most of the time…

Laurie Darter—thank you for your honest feedback of #TLS, your fantastic company, and Magic Mike XL; your gift of half-naked men dancing on the big screen is something I will never forget. Mostly because it burned my retina's, and caused me to laugh when no one else in the theater was except you and Christine…

Christine Kuttnauer—who became a sounding board on this project after helping me tie up *A Kiss Like This* with a tidy little bow. Every time I open a private message online and start laughing, tears streaming out of my eyes, my husband asks "What is so damn funny?"

It's usually you. Or you and Shirl, together.

You have an amazing eye for the little details that make a huge impact; and incredible ideas for storylines. I particularly love the plot line involving mud wrestling and stolen kisses, although I'll have to be creative about working that one into my next book. Or was it kisses in the rain with some mud? Or just kissing.

Dammit Christine, make up your mind!

I don't think you hear often enough about how remarkable you are; how talented and clever and wonderful. I am so grateful to call you my friend.

Special thanks to Wendi Temporado—may this be the beginning of a long, beautiful relationship.

Jennifer Cashin, Kirstin Kanoff, the real Abby Darlington, and Chandler Kadlec, for loving this book before it was even edited.

And as always, thank you to all my readers.

Every day I try to improve my writing, and dream up stories: for you.